CONTENTS

DARKNESS FALLS

BETHANI BRIANNA   PAUL EAGLE   R. J. ERBACHER

HENRY VINICIO VALERIO MADRIZ   BOB MCNEIL

WILLIAM JOHN ROSTRON   ELAINE GILMARTIN

BRADLEY H. SINOR   LIAM A SPINAGE

BRIAN STIEGLITZ   KELLY ZIMMER

FOREWARD

"When you crest the distant rise and you come upon Darkness Falls, you see the town laid out before you in a flat floored valley, usually shrouded in haze. Drawing closer, a collection of unbecoming rectangular buildings can be seen, gray or brown with little character. The town, once beautiful, actually did have a waterfall, an abundant river crashing over the ridge to the north and depositing into a wide lake. But no one alive remembers back that far and the river has long since run dry. Early on there was nothing more than a couple of dozen farms and a white clapboard chapel with a peculiar rood atop its steeple. But as the place grew, an ordinance was changed allowing a steel factory to be built, in the hopes of revitalizing the struggling economy. Other businesses followed. The amount of people that filtered in for work was more than the local boarding houses could handle and apartment buildings were soon constructed. From that point on Darkness Falls deteriorated into an urban complex, complete with crime, unrest and desperation. Sections fell into dilapidated slums while others teetered on the fringe of sustenance, trying vainly to hold onto their crumbling worth. Now there are as many abandoned buildings as viable ones and there are few remnants of the little community of homes that once thrived along its winding roads. Nobody stays long in

Darkness Falls; the companies, the tenants, even the vagrants. There are only a few permanent residents that linger here, people you wouldn't want to meet on the hollow streets at night. The one constant is the darkness that at some point overcomes everyone and everything. And there are strange occurrences in that darkness. Things that most people wouldn't want to experience even in their dreams. Some recover and move on. Some never escape. Whatever the reason that your travels bring you into Darkness Falls your best option is to keep going. Do not stop for food or gas or lodging. Unfortunately, some do and they find out that the town stays true to its name. There is always the darkness…"

WASTED WATER

R. J. ERBACHER

Damn, Jamie wanted to take a relaxing shower this morning. A nice soak in the steamy spray, hot water swirling endlessly into the drain, as he stood there doing nothing. That would have been enjoyable. But he was running late and decided the most prudent course was to skip his usual daily ablutions and head into the office. Now, sitting in his car for these six some hours, he was regretting it as his skin felt itchy beneath his three-piece suit. To make up for it he decided on an extra-long shower tonight.

He only worked a half day at his desk, finishing up some paperwork, because he had the long drive ahead of him and he wanted to get to Darkness Falls before night. His GPS readout stated that he had twenty more minutes until he reached his destination and the sun was already settling behind the mountain ridge to the west. So, it would be dark when he reached Darkness Falls. Ironic, or maybe prophetic. Possibly poetic. Or even prognostic. Cataloging synonyms; the things that occupied your mind on long trips.

His boss had put him in charge of finding a building in an inconspicuous location where they could finalize production of his company's knock-off semiconductors. The majority of computer wafers, as they were called, were made in Taiwan, South Korea and China but a good number were still produced in the good old US of A and the move to 'Made in America' products continued to increase Perditio Components' stock. The situation was this: semiconductors needed to be cleaned with water many times to ensure the high standards of proper delineation, over two thousand gallons of water were required for a single thirty-centimeter wafer. Their main operations were all in California and the restrictions there on water had become continually more stringent. They had to find an out-of-the-way facility to ship the components where they could waste vast quantities of water to clean the wafers in the final production. Someplace where the squander wouldn't be noticed by hungry media or EPA dilettantes. Enter Darkness Falls.

An urban hole in the wall with lots of unoccupied buildings that were waiting to be snatched up for a song. A place nobody cared about and few people even knew existed. Was even said to have a haunted mansion in the middle of it someplace. But through some intense online searching he had found the town, which oddly enough had a history of water vanishing as the falls of Darkness Falls had mysteriously dried up over a hundred plus years ago. So, nobody was going to care about a little more water running down the drain. The cherry on the cake was this perfect building to suit their purposes. And the price was astoundingly low. Now all he had to do was check out the location to make sure it would satisfy their needs and he'd be a hero.

Flying was preferable, and Perditio would have picked up the tab, but the closest airport was a two-and-a-half-hour drive from Darkness Falls and the amount of time he would have expended in the cab to the airport, arriving early, going through security, flying, waiting at the rental agency, coupled with the trip in the car from the airport to where he was going and traffic made it more feasible to just drive the whole way. From his office, all six plus hours of it. Thinking back now, maybe not such a smart idea.

On top of that, he'd had an argument with his secretary about where he was going to stay. A trip this long required at least an overnight stay and he wanted one of the better hotel chains where he could get a comfortable bed, some decent grub and a good shower. But because the town was in the middle of nowhere, the only thing she could find meant he would have to drive an additional forty-five miles past Darkness Falls to reach the nearest one. Not such a big deal but when you're already over six hours in the car he didn't want to push it to seven. Reluctantly Jamie agreed to her suggestion which was to stay at a motor court in the town itself, apparently, they didn't have hotels, but it was just a few minutes' drive from the factory's location so he would make do. He dreaded the accommodations he would have to endure but he put it out of his head. For one night Jamie would sacrifice comfort for convenience.

The dusk was fading into evening as he pulled into town past rotting fields of corn. The name epitomized the area because when the sun set, the curtain of night came down with an abrupt finality; darkness fell with a resounding crash. As he drove through another synonym came to mind, treacherous. The place in the dark looked none too inviting.

Jamie pulled into the Darkness Falls Motel. Twenty rooms painted dull blue, horseshoed around a cracked asphalt parking lot with fading lines. This did not look promising he thought giving the place a once over as he stretched the kinks out of his back and legs. The lobby office was no better. A glass front with a single unoccupied but cluttered desk and a plaque hanging from a suction cup on the door that read 'Open.' Entering set off a chime and Jamie perused as he waited for someone to respond. There was a vinyl couch with rusting steel arms, a dusty plastic floor plant and a water vending machine with an 'out of order' sign taped to it and no bottles inside. He could have used a water right about now. A half minute later a beer bellied man with a week untouched growth on his face came out from the back. The sound of a television filter out from the inner room that was almost inaudible, but he thought it might have been the moaning and groaning of porn.

"Can I help you?"

"Yes, I have a reservation. Jamie Iblis."

The clerk looked his business suit up and down with disdain then flipped a few pages of a book that was hidden from view behind the counter. His eyes came up for a second then returned to the book.

"Sorry, no reservations by that name," he said.

"You sure? Iblis, I-B-L-I-S. Maybe under the company name, Perditio Components. My secretary made them yesterday and secured them with my credit card," Jamie huffed out.

With only a cursory glance back down and another page turn he responded simply, "Nope."

"Fine. Can I just get a room for the night? Whatever you have." Jamie's annoyance meter was starting to red line.

"Sorry, we're full up."

Jamie's eyes almost bulged from his skull. He turned and looked to the lot outside and then shot back pointing that way.

"There are only three cars in the parking lot and one of them is mine. You're trying to tell me you don't have a single room available for the night? Please, check again. "

Through gritted teeth the guy spoke distinctly, leaning forward, "I am the manager ,sir and I don't have to check again. I know what's available in my own motel and I'm telling you we have no vacancy and no reservation for you. Now, is there anything else I can help you with?"

Jamie, not one to back down from a threat, brought his face up to the clerks matching his vocal tremor.

"Is there any other place in this town where a person might find a room?" The word 'town' came out as if it were an insult.

"I don't know. Why don't you drive around and find out?"

Jamie decided to give up the battle. There did not appear to be an upside to continuing the exchange. He wasn't getting a bed and shower here, maybe just as well. He turned on his heels and headed out, stopping at the entrance to turn the sign around so 'Closed' face out. He slammed the door and then drove away. A few blocks later he pulled into a gas station to fill up.

He tried inserting his credit card a couple of times into the slot but it didn't register. He walked over to the booth where a young kid who was close enough in appearance that he might have been the motel manager's son, peered out through hooded eyes.

"The card's not going through," Jamie said.

"Cash only." It seemed a great burden to have to relay this information.

Jamie had only been in this town for less than half an hour and he already hated all of it and everybody. He pulled his wallet and slid a twenty through the slot which the kid snatched. Then seeing a glass reach-in refrigerator behind the attendant that was covered with stick on advertising, produced another five and asked for a bottle of water. He suddenly realized how thirsty he was.

"No water."

"What? It's the single most purchased drink in the world and you don't have any?"

"No water," the attendant repeated as if on a recorded loop.

"What's in the cooler?" Jamie asked a little too forcefully.

"Beer, orange juice. And beer."

"Give me an orange juice."

"We're out of orange juice."

Jamie pulled his five back and spit out, "Just the gas, then." He took a breath to compose himself and continued. "Is there any place nearby to get a room?"

"The Motor Court, couple of blocks back."

"Yeah, I tried there but they're full."

"Really." There was something in the way the kid said that word and the smile that followed that didn't sit well with Jamie. The attendant started going on, saying something about some boarding houses on the outskirts of town that were still in operation and that some of them might have lodging, but he decided right then and there that he wasn't staying at someone's creepy house that might have a woodshed in back filled with some chainsaws. He wouldn't spend even one night in this town. If he could help it.

Jamie mumbled an acknowledgement and filled up his tank. Sitting there in his car under the muted lights of the station he puzzled out his dilemma. He could bite the bullet and drive the additional forty-five minutes to the hotel that was his original accommodation idea. Or he could find a place to park and sleep in his car and wait for morning to look at the building and then head back tomorrow. Both were not high on his list of solutions but the bucket-seat-bed seemed the worst of the two. Waking up stiff and uncomfortable for having slept in his clothes and especially not getting his long sought-after shower he would be miserable and that would be a prelude to an aggravating ride home. Besides he doubted if there was a safe enough area in Darkness Falls where he could keep his car where he wouldn't get attacked or vandalized. He was still worrying out his options when a sound explosion from the rear nearly had him jumping through the windshield. A monster of a pickup truck had pulled in behind him and having waited all of a second and a half for his car to move away from the pump, had given a blast of an air horn that was probably appropriated from a tug boat. Jamie calmed his pounding heart and put his car into gear.

He pulled up to the next stop light and gazed around while waiting for the green signal. This city was really depressing. A good many of the small shops were boarded up or had soaped windows. The ones that were operating did not have a welcoming appearance. The road was mostly empty and few cars were either parked or running up and down what appeared to be the main drag. There weren't more than a handful of people walking about either. Even the street lights had a dull sodium glow that was more hazy yellow than white and did little to light up the town. Jamie was thankful he didn't have to live here. Just check the stupid factory and be done with this place.

Then a thought occurred to him. Why did he have to wait until morning to inspect the factory? True, in the dark of night, and it was really dark, there were things he wouldn't be able to see on the outside of the structure but aesthetics was not really a huge concern. He could care less how the building looked to the average passerby. In fact, a nondescript appearance was actually in its favor. As long as the inside offered what the company required for the spraying of the semiconductors that would be all they needed. And he could check that at any time, day or night. Mr. Acheron, the landlord, who had overnighted him a set of keys to get in, had assured him that the electricity was still on so he could go there right now, give the place the once over and be gone from this shithole of a town. With no traffic and maybe a couple dozen cups of coffee he could be back in his own bed before the sun came up and since he already had tomorrow off could sleep the whole day. He would be too tired arriving home to shower so he'd have to wait until tomorrow night when he woke and although going more than forty-eight hours without washing up was personally revolting, he would live with it if it meant getting the hell out of Darkness Falls. At last, he had a plan.

Pulling to the curb on the next block he punched the address of the building into his GPS and saw he was less than ten minutes from the location. Perfect. Get there, get 'er done, get out.

In the short drive there, the scenery didn't change much. A couple of apartment buildings that could have been relatively new but still looked run down at the same time, some other gray factories that either were fully functional or abandoned, he couldn't really tell, and more gloomily lit streets. There was a dented sign pointing down a pot-holed road that said 'Civic Center.' He passed a bar called 'The Watering Hole' that was roped off with a spider web of yellow crime scene tape, one more reason not to stay. The Darkness Falls Police Station looked as run down as Racoon City's from the video game. Jamie registered it all with as little acknowledgement as possible. He didn't have to come up with a publicity package to sell the town to his boss. Only the building. The four main concerns were that it had facilities enough to clean the wafers with water, it had access to unload and reload shipments, the place was off the beaten path yet still close enough to California that trucks could drive there in about a day or so. The last two boxes were already ticked off, he just needed to verify the first two. He could probably do that in less than half an hour with some pictures and his job would be done. Jamie's confidence was high as he turned into the parking lot behind the gargantuan brick edifice. There was one other car in the lot. The shell of an SUV that looked like it had not survived a car bombing in Beirut. He parked several spots away from it.

Standing next to his open car door, just in case something should threaten him in the dark and he needed to jump back inside and go tearing away, Jamie located a short staircase that led up to a brown metal door. This is the door the manager had told him about and sent the keys for. Just as he beeped the car alarm he was startled by the sound of a gruff, loud voice.

"You can't be here!"

"What?" Jamie looked around for the source of the sound.

"This is my place."

A crumpled old man flopped out of a pillage of tarps and newspapers from the back of the burnt car. His clothes and coat were grease stained and tattered, two different type boots on his feet. A wool cap with a rip in it was plastered onto his head, a tuft of gray hair sticking up from the hole. He groaned himself up into a standing hunch and coughed and spat out a wad of phlegm.

"Your place?" Jamie questioned.

"That's right. My place."

"So, you must be the landlord Mr. Acheron," Jamie said, blending sarcasm and superiority.

"Who the hell is that?" The disheveled man wandered about gazing down as if he'd lost something.

"Mr. Acheron is the person who sent me the keys to that door right there, told me I could park here and go in and examine his building. Since you're not him I'm guessing this is not your place. Unless of course you're the mayor of Darkness Falls?"

"I might as well be, damn it. Nobody has lived here longer than old Doyle. And if I say this is my place, you best believe it." His eyes with a momentary ferocity in them, finally came up to meet Jamie's. The look passed between them, then dissolved.

"I'll tell you what, Doyle. If you watch my car for the next half hour and make sure nothing happens to it, when I come out to leave, I'll give you ten bucks. How does that sound?"

Doyle swung his head from side-to-side mumbling to himself before exclaiming, "Make it twenty."

"How about I make it ten and let's say I won't call the police and have you removed." This exchange was getting on Jamie's nerves and he was already near the fraying point.

"Police? Ha, ha, ha. Good luck with that."

Jamie didn't like the sound of his statement. It didn't appear to be a bluff. It was the confidence of someone who knew what he was talking about from experience. From his view of the seemingly unoccupied station earlier he could understand.

"Ok, fifteen dollars, but you make sure a bird doesn't so much as shit on my car."

"No birds around here, not at night. Other things. Other things at night."

Other things? He liked the implication of that even less than the police remark. Jamie's notion to hightail it from here sooner than later was becoming more prudent. He shook off the chill that went through him and gestured to Doyle. "We have a deal?"

After a pause Doyle said, "Deal. Shake on it."

"No. That's OK, I'll take you at your word. Half an hour."

Doyle nodded. Jamie went up the concrete stairs holding the steel pipe railing which rattled in its berth. Just as he went to the door, he heard from behind him, "Be vigilant" He turned back to the sound of Doyle's voice but couldn't see the old man standing anywhere. Maybe he crawled back into his refuse bundle in the back of the SUV skeleton. Whatever.

Jamie used two keys that had been sent to him by Mr. Acheron to unlock the industrial steel door. One was a regular door latch but the other was a fox style double bolt lock. The kind with a knob in the middle that rolled out two steel bars in opposing directions to secure the door as surely as a dungeon cross beam. He wondered what had been so important here that they had to keep it so protected from anyone entering. With a little cajoling he managed to get the door untethered and pushed in. A tentative peak behind him at the lot outside, still not seeing Doyle, and he could now easily understand the extra security measures. Inside he rotated the bolts back in place, the confidence of their grinding clang abating his uneasiness. Jamie lit up his phone and looked for a light switch. Eventually he found it up a half flight of stairs and inside the main entrance to the factory floor. A whole bank of switches that gradually illuminated the empty space as he flipped each one on. Some came on fully, others dully hummed and a few not at all. The place was huge.

The first thing Jamie noticed was a scattering of edged metal fragments. There were no tables or assembly lines, just an open area, a few drum size garbage bins and a couple of rough wood pallets with no loads. But all over the floor were silver metallic palm-sized scraps that looked like punch outs from a sheet metal press. Mr. Acheron never mentioned to him what had been manufactured here previously so these scraps were curious. He stepped over to the nearest one and picked it up and promptly cut his finger. It resembles the symbol that the artist formerly known as Prince used in his transformation phase but it was not that elegant. Not intentionally he was sure, but it almost had a satanic design as he examined it for a moment, all of the others about him appearing to be exactly the same shape, same wicked sharpness. Jamie discarded it and sucked the blood from the small cut on the end of his thumb, assessing the rest of the interior. There were high window panes that ran the length of one wall, some were shattered, not broken, as they were inlaid with wire mesh. Puddles lay in three or four spots punctuating the location where the roof would need repairing. Some crumbling cement beams, jungle vine wires and lots of rusty pipes, besides dust and cobwebs. Mostly minor stuff that came with all old buildings but since he was getting it for dirt cheap, he could live with the little annoyances. The place hadn't been condemned; it was just abandoned and needed an industrial cleaning.

The thing that thrilled him particularly was all of the metal grills located throughout the expanse. Slotted floor plates that lead to an underground drainage system that would collect the waste water they would be using to clean the wafers. There were probably two dozen of them strategically located about the building so multiple stations could be utilized. That was the selling point for this location. The overflow would slush away into the sewer pipes underneath and to wherever waste water went. Jamie didn't know or care. So far everything looked great.

A quick spin of the floor, careful of where he stepped, taking snapshots with his phone from every angle to certify he'd made the right choice. There were more highlighted places he still had to check out. There was supposedly a warehouse in back, a dock area with three rollup doors for truck unloading, a boiler room, the employee lounge and lunch room. A priority was also testing that the water lines were working and abundant, but the thing that caught his interest straight away was the manager's office overhead. The ceilings were eighteen to twenty feet high and up against the roof at the right side of the layout was an office that overlooked the factory floor, a long staircase against the wall that led up to it. The treehouse structure was definitely an add on, installed for its strategic view. Constructed of wood with four-by-four beams that precariously held it aloft and a wall of glass windows it was the location where the manager could watch out from his turret like an overseer and observe that no one was goofing off or stealing merchandise or just up to no good. The onus of the parapet kind of excited him.

Each stair groaned as he placed his shoe upon it. In a noisy factory din the sound probably went unnoticed but the whines that echoed in the hollow emptiness were ominous. At the top there was a door that was not locked and next to it a couple of switches. He flicked them on. Inside the room was split into two. As soon as you stepped in there was a makeshift conference room, only half lit working fluorescent lights, where a scratched rectangular table stood with no chairs around it. Then a sliding door cordoned off a small office, the lighting in here even worse than the previous space. A desk with all the drawers removed, an open closet with wrecked shelving and another small door in the corner. Jamie walked on the threadbare brown carpeting that covered the plank flooring towards the windows that overlooked the factory. He cringed with the creak of the structure and halted a few paces from the edge. Better not push his luck. From this vantage the space below appeared twice as large. He turned about-face. The room had been emptied out by the last occupants but again was not destroyed or defaced in any way. He took a chance at the last door expecting some kind of storage. He was shocked to find a small bathroom. A single bulb that hung from a wire snaked out of the ceiling and popped on with the switch. An airplane lavatory sink, crammed next to a toilet rimmed with brown water stains and no seat and a phone booth shower. He looked it once over and absently reached for the shower handle and turned it. To his surprise a spray came streaming out with a surprisingly good flow. Well, the place had water. Again, mostly out of curiosity he let it run. The water which started out opaque brown quickly diluted to clear, swirled and went down the drain without any blockage. He took some pics of the bathroom, the two rooms and one out the windows at the area below and came back to the running shower. Putting his hand in, the water had become satisfyingly warm. Whatever hot water system that was in the building had not been turned off. This presented him with an opportunity.

He wasn't going to sleep tonight, that was no biggie; he'd pulled all-nighters before for many reasons. But how much better would the ride home be if he could get a shower, even a fast one. Feel refreshed, invigorated and symbolically cleansed of this place. Maybe not the most hygienic of places to wash up but he had brought his own towels in his luggage, as he always did because hotel towels usually sucked, and he could lay one down on the plastic base to protect his feet. Five minutes in and out and he would be a new man. Jamie mulled it over for another sixty seconds and decided to go for it. The best of a bad situation.

He jogged down the stairs, their protests as loud as before, unlocked the steel door and went out to his car. Not surprisingly as he took in the parking lot, Doyle was nowhere to be seen. Well, the vagrant could forget the fifteen bucks. Bending into his trunk he unzipped his travel bag, pulled out clean pants, shirt, underwear and socks, his two luxurious bath towels, ultra-soft and absorbent, and his dopp kit. There were some plastic bags he had shoved in the corner next to his ice scraper for emergencies and he took a couple to put his dirty clothes and soggy towels in. With the car locked back up he double checked that nothing was out of the ordinary and headed back inside, locked the security door and sprinted back to the manager's office.

Tossing the contents of his pockets up on the desktop; keys, wallet, change, money clip, and phone, Janie then proceed to strip, laying out his soiled clothes, and put his clean clothes neatly over them so they wouldn't get dusty, his shoes next to it all on the corner and marched buck-ass into the bathroom with his towels and kit. He closed the door and immersed himself in the shower. The warm splash on his face, cascading down his body was heavenly. He used his travel bottle of body wash to soap up from head to toes and then shut his eyes and stepped into the stream to let the dirt and scum rinse away. If he had his druthers Jamie would have lingered in this position for ten or fifteen minutes letting the water strip away his annoyances of the day, but he knew he had to cut it short. A quick hair scrub and he'd be done. When he opened his eyes to grab his tube of shampoo he was in total darkness.

Great. The sole bulb must have burnt out. Fumbling around blindly he reached out of the shower stall searching for the bathroom door handle. It took four or five passes but he managed to snag the knob and pushed the door open. No light filtered in from the next room. Not so much as a sliver of dullness. It was stone cold black. Maybe a fuse blew? But why didn't he see some ambient light from the factory floor shining through the large office windows. Could the electricity for the whole building have suddenly gone out? This was not good. Really not good. He shut the water off and searched for his dry towel. It was draped over the sink he thought but in the inviolable blackness he could not find a sense of direction, or the sink. His feet tangled in the towel he'd laid down in the base of the shower and he went down hard, out onto the floor, banging his knees and elbows.

"Shit!"

Forget the towel, he had to get his phone. That would give him some light and he'd could find his bearings, get dried and dressed and decide what to do next. Jamie began crawling from the bathroom through the door into the office in the direction that he thought the desk might be. It was scary how dark it was. Almost like he'd been blindfolded even though his eyes were spread wide and primed for some sign of light. Moving on two knees and one hand, the other arm swiping in front of him like an insect antenna, trying not to bang into anything while also probing for the side of the desk. Grit and dust from the carpet were collecting all over his wet legs and hands and he'd need another shower just to clean up from this debacle. The groan of the wood as he proceeded was downright terrifying now as the whole structure seemed to be secured with nothing more than spit and duct tape. Low to the floor like this Jamie could feel the sway more pronounced as he moved. The plywood between the beams bowed far more than it should have as he went forward. Where the hell was the goddamn desk?

His flailing hand finally contacted with something solid but it wasn't the desk but the wall with the windows that peered down at the factory floor. Had he gone too far right or left? Jamie pulled himself up to the touch of the glass on his hand until he felt the pane against his chin and nose. Even with all the electricity off he should still be able to see some light from the street lamps outside through the upper windows, unless the whole town had blacked out. If that, then what about the moon and stars? This absence of any light was baffling. How could he see absolutely nothing? Jamie put his back against the wall, dropped his bare ass onto the rug and tried to logically figure this out.

This was not a natural darkness. Had he gone temporarily blind? He would think that incidents of sudden blindness would incur a head impact or eye injury. That didn't happen. How would a person even check that? Look at something that for certain you knew had light. The only thing he knew for sure in his immediate capacity would be his cell phone. It was well charged and he had used it just a few minutes ago so it was working. Now all he had to do was find the desk. How to do that? The room was small enough that it should be easy. The desk was near the center of the room. If he had his back to one wall and he went either left or right he would come to a corner. With his one hand on a wall and his other on the adjoining wall he could find a diagonal direction which would bisect the room and bring him to the desk. Simple enough.

Jamie stood up and leaned his butt against the cold glass plate. He arbitrarily decided to shuffle to the right, his palms flat for guidance. With each step the creaking of the floor seemed to intensify, sending shivers through his spine. After a few paces he suddenly felt no resistance against his back and a breeze on his bare skin. An instant later the glass panel that he'd leaned against crashed into a shattering eruption on the stone floor below. He was dangling in space. He reached out for the first thing and grabbed the glass panel next to the one that had fallen out. It gave him momentary support before it pulled free of its frame and also tumbled away. Jamie had such a grip on the window that when it fell it pulled him down with it. The wall that braced up the pane cracked off when he struck it with his torso and he went through. Grappling for anything he managed to get both hands on the floor plywood while his body dangled down in midair. The impact of his fall and the weakened structure without its windows shuddered the whole construction and cross beam two-by-fours pulled free of their securement and the base bucked sideways. With the wood broken free the only thing his white-knuckled fists were holding was the edge of the carpet and the sound of tearing rug was the indignity that finally made him scream.

The carpet ripped downward for a stretch of about six feet before coming loose altogether and he was in freefall. Two seconds after that he landed on his back, smacking against the cement floor of the factory and rolling a few times. Jamie felt pain in a couple of places at once. His muscles in his legs and back were throbbing from the impact and then there were these stinging pains in his legs, thighs, arms, chest and back. When he finally came to a stop, his hands splayed to cease the body flipping, he still could not see a speck. Slowly he began probing his exterior wounds and discovered what the agony to his skin was. One of the sharp metallic punchouts of the demonic symbols was sticking out of his bicep. He pulled it free and felt a warm stream of blood running down his arm. He had nine or ten gashes on his torso from the steel shivs. His hands were slippery and sticky and he could only imagine what kind of horror show he must resemble. The rest of the aches hurt a lot and would hurt more in the morning, if there was a morning left in his future. Nothing was broken and he was able to unsteadily stand but once he was upright, he realized he didn't have a clue to where he was, which way to go, and most importantly, what to do next.

He took one tentative step and slashed the bottom of his foot on another one of the metal scraps and went back down to his knees only to catch another one there and bounced howling over to his side. The damn things were everywhere. Easily spotted in the light, in the darkness they became a landmine obstacle course. Jamie whimpered out his frustrations and was not more than an instant away from tears when he felt something else. Something much worse.

A furry creature brushed across his stomach, past his groin and down along his leg in a fast scramble, the ticking of tiny claws heading away from him. Now he let out a little feminine yelp. A rat, and by no means a little one, in fact a might sizable one from the feel of it, scurried off and stopped at a short distance away. Maybe it wasn't a rat, but definitely a large rodent-like animal. Whatever it was he heard another one behind him. With no lights to dissuade them, they were coming out of the woodwork. He sensed skittering around him in multiple directions. Jamie ambled up to his knees and began waving his arms, making strange noises he never made before in the hopes of keeping them at bay. They were within striking distance he felt, although none approached to investigate him further. He heard them close by, too close, guessing they smelt his leaking bodily fluids and were looking for a quick meal. How much blood was he losing? The minute he stopped moving they would be on him.

Deliberating on his plan of action was no longer an option. He had to move. In a ridiculous parade of motion, he tenderly searched in front of him for steel impediments, when that was clear he scuttled a few paces forward on his knees, flung his arms with a yell to dispel the creatures and then repeated the whole process again. For three minutes he did that with a dread that he had not made any progress toward somewhere helpful. Catching his breath, a new terror assaulted his ears.

A slow grating of metal on metal, of a plate sliding free of its moorings. Jamie tried to think what the nearby sound could be. The only thing that he could come up with were the grills that dotted the floor and would be used to collect runoff water. But tiny paws couldn't be moving those, no matter how big the wooly vermin were. Unless the grates were being pushed up from underneath. The only thing below the metallic framework was drain piping. What could be coming up from the sewers? Jamie didn't know exactly what, and wasn't sure he wanted to know yet when a scaley appendage slithered over the back of his legs, he flung his body in the opposite direction from the repulsion. A low-pitched hiss/growl/croak issued from nearby and moved into a circular path around him. His murky mind projected the image of an elongated belly-dragging, tail-wagging slink, a grotesque cross between a lizard and a shark with a maw full of teeth. He followed the sonance with his ears as it went, his open palm stretched defensively outward. As if his hand was worth losing over anything else. What the bejesus was it and how did it ascend from the cesspit of hell? And then it went silent which immediately seemed more petrifying in the dark than hearing it. Until he caught the chilling scratch of another grill being slid aside to his right. And another left.

His body started to tremble. Jamie was cold, wet, dirty, bloodied, bruised, thirsty, frightened and lost. He was being stalked by the 'other things' Doyle had spoken about that came out at night. He was without his keys, wallet or phone, and his clothes. Defenseless and naked. And he was still shrouded in utter darkness. All he could think to do was shout, even though he knew it was a futile gesture.

"Help!"

Jamie repeated it several times, each louder and more desperate. He was full out crying now, tears running down his face, dripping to the floor. Wasted water.

Had he been about to die in either the electric chair or a firing squad he would be scared but at least his fate would have a conclusion. A finality, albeit not a happy one. This was so much worse for he had no idea where to go. What was about to happen to him. How much pain he was about to endure. He had given up hope of an escape. He had just given up hope. Jamie curled into a fetal position bawling hysterically. For the first time since he was a kid he prayed. Prayed for an ending. One that wouldn't be awful.

Clicking claws and slithering slime seemed to be closing in on him, now unnaturally loud. Maybe God would have pity on him, give him a heart attack or just take him up to heaven in a beam of penetrating white light. In a fantasy movie, maybe. Not in Darkness Falls. In Darkness Falls you got Doyle.

"I told you to be vigilant." The sound reverberated in the cavernous space. Jamie had sucked in his mewling with a gasp at the startling clear tone of Doyle's statement. Suddenly there were no other noises about him. As if Doyle had made them instantly vanish into the blackness. Or had they been there at all? He couldn't tell where Doyle was, his voice seemed to be everywhere at once.

"Your car's safe. Where's my money?"

"Help me, please." Jamie didn't bother to even raise his head. What if Doyle was just in his imagination as well? Maybe this was all a nightmare. Could he be that lucky?

"Help you? Get up!"

The toe of Doyle's boot caught him in the ribs, assuring him that this was no dream. Jamie managed to get somewhat straight but still cringing in his dark world.

"I-I can't see."

"That's cause it's dark here. Or didn't you know that about this place? The name not give you a clue!" Doyle's bad breath was now right in his face and he sensed him close enough to take a bite out of him if he had the inclination, which at this point wouldn't be out of the realm of possibility.

"I need to...," Jamie spluttered.

"Yeah, yeah. You need to get out of here."

Doyle's hand clamped onto the back of his neck with a ferocious grip he never expected from the old man and began pushing and steering Jamie in a direction. Each step he anticipated impaling his sole onto one of those discarded metal barbs or being bitten by a rat or reptile but he was being ushered in a clear path. It seemed like Jamie walked very far, very quickly and suddenly he was stumbling down steps. The grinding sound of the rolling bolt lock pinpointed where he exactly was. With a clang the door opened and he was shoved out into the cold, lit world of the parking lot.

Jamie saw light. Street lights. Moon glow. Star twinkles. Passing car headlights on the elevated highway in the distance. Window lights from surrounding buildings. And when he turned to look back at Doyle the illuminated factory through the open door behind his rescuer. He tried to utter something but nothing came out.

"Here."

Doyle tossed him his car keys and he caught them against his bare chest. Jamie looked up in bewilderment. How did Doyle get in? How did he find him in the darkness? How did he get his keys? What the hell was happening? He looked down at the fob in his hand and realized he was naked. Most of his body splotched with dried blood smears and black dirt. Jamie gazed up at Doyle ignoring the illogical aspects of the whole evening.

"What about my things? My clothes, phone and wallet?"

Doyle looked oddly at him. "Do you really want to come back in and get them?"

Jamie started to shiver uncontrollably but quickly answered, "No."

"Didn't think so." It was now Doyle's turn to size Jamie up and stare scornfully at him. "You're a mess, man. Go home and take a shower."

Jamie thought that was a perfect idea. He padded down the stone steps in his bare feet, chirped his car, jumped in and drove away as fast as he could manage. When he was far away from here, he would worry about everything else. Now he just needed to put distance between himself and Darkness Falls.

Doyle watched him drive away. He said out loud, to no one in particular, "I told you this was my place."

THE END

SLUMBER PARTY

KELLY ZIMMER

Charlotte shouldered her backpack and shouted curses at the driver who'd given her a lift. She'd been grateful for the ride until he put his hands on her the moment they stopped. The guy in the ball cap apologized and backed off, but Charlotte wasn't getting back in that pickup truck.

Her shouts carried over the roar of diesel engines to the next pump. Kevin Bradshaw didn't intervene but, as the dad of two teenage girls, he felt compelled to watch out for the kid in case the guy got rough, but she seemed to handle things. He watched the girl stomp into the truck stop's service center. The driver didn't follow, and drove off before she returned.

Kevin finished fueling up, then parked his rig off to the side. It was after two, and though he still had four hundred miles to cover, he needed a break and some food. He spotted the girl working on a hamburger outside a fast-food stand in the service center. She attacked her sandwich and fries with enthusiasm, unconcerned about her ride taking off without her, so he turned his attention to the menu board.

After lunch, Kevin returned to his rig, where the girl, still hanging around, approached him as he climbed into the cab.

"Please, mister, can you give me a lift out of here?"

She had a sweet smile set in a heart-shaped face, honey blonde hair cut in a pixie, and startling blue-green eyes. The kid was adorable and vulnerable.

"How old are you, kid?" he asked.

The smile fell. "Eighteen."

"Bullshit. You know how dangerous hitching a ride is? I've got two girls your age at home. They'd never get in a truck with a stranger."

The sweetness vanished. "I don't need a lecture; I just need a ride. You planning on raping me?"

"No, but the next guy might."

"Well, you'd better give me a lift first, hadn't you?" Violet-tinted lips curled in a teasing grin.

Kevin grunted and shook his head. "Git in."

She was sixteen and ran away because her stepdad was a dick, and her mother didn't give a shit about anything but booze and reality shows. That's about all Kevin learned in the three hours they rode together.

Though the girl talked non-stop, she said little. Having endured the manic teen experience firsthand, Kevin listened and didn't press for details. His only concerns were staying on schedule and dropping the kid somewhere safe.

As the shadows lengthened, Charlotte shifted in her seat. Kevin wasn't sure if she had to pee or was spooked by the fading light.

"You need a rest break?" he asked.

"Yeah. When's the next town?"

It was Kevin's turn to squirm. The next town they'd reach would be Darkness Falls. He stopped there once, and that was enough. "Five miles, but if you wait thirty minutes, the next place has better facilities."

The truck's cab seemed to close in around her and Charlotte craved escape. *Here we go again.* In thirty minutes, it would be dark. She hadn't considered where she'd spend the night, but in a truck with another handsy stranger wasn't part of the plan.

"Next stop is fine," she said. "Do they have a hotel?"

"Geez Louise, no! You're not spending the night in Darkness Falls."

The blood left Charlotte's face as panic set in. "Look, mister, thanks for the ride, but I'm not spending the night in your truck."

Kevin raised a palm. "Just until the next town. Look, you got a cell phone? Pull it out and punch in nine-one. If I make a move, hit the one again and call the cops."

Charlotte had forgotten to recharge her phone at the truck stop, and doubted it had much juice left. The guy didn't know that, so she could fake it, but she really needed to pee.

"Drop me off at the next town, or I'll call the cops and scream rape."

Kevin wanted to bang his head against the windshield. He couldn't leave the idiot kid in Darkness Falls. He wouldn't leave a dead dog in that place, but he had his family to consider. An arrest would devastate them. It wasn't fair to put his wife and girls through that, not for a flighty kid who enjoyed pushing her luck.

"Fine," he said.

They drove the rest of the way in silence. Kevin didn't pull his rig onto the patchwork road leading into Darkness Falls, just eased to the side of the highway.

Charlotte's breath caught when Kevin reached for the glove box.

"Relax, I'm going for my wallet." He kept one eye on her as he extracted two tens and a five. "There's an inn. Nineteen-ninety-five a night and get yourself some dinner."

"I've got money," she protested.

"Save it for bus fare to get your ass home."

"Stop lecturing me!" Charlotte snatched the bills from his hand and climbed from the cab.

Kevin watched as she strode off in the gloom. In Darkness Falls, it was already night.

The couple of diners stared bug-eyed when the creaky door banged behind Charlotte. Their silence and questioning eyes made the fine hairs on the back of her neck prickle, but she kept a dignified pace as she strode to the short hall leading to the restrooms.

The bathroom was clean except for the corners and smelled okay except for the mold and Charlotte emerged with restored confidence. She chose a table smack in the middle of the nearly empty diner and snatched a paper menu from between the salt and pepper shakers. She studied it for five minutes before the hefty African American guy behind the counter approached her table.

"Meatloaf, onion rings, and a Coke." She tossed the menu aside.

The guy disappeared through an arch to the kitchen. Her dinner arrived ten minutes later, fresh from the microwave, nothing home-made about it. The onion rings were limp, and the meatloaf was cold in the center. Even her mom's cooking was better, but she ate it. The guy returned to refill her Coke and leave a handwritten bill on the table. He hovered, and Charlotte guessed he was waiting for his money.

She tossed one of Kevin's tens toward him, then watched the big guy punch it in at the old register at the counter. Though she had slept little, and none of it in a proper bed, twenty bucks for a room at the Darkness Falls Inn seemed out of the question. With her cash dwindling, she needed a free place to crash.

After the counter guy returned with her change, she dawdled over her drink, wondering if she could hide in the restroom and spend the night in the diner. Probably not. It wasn't like she could get lost in the crowd in this dump.

Charlotte massaged her forehead with her fingertips to fight off the fatigue and hopelessness. She'd been on the run for three days, was nearly broke, and needed a shower. Oh, and her phone was dead.

She glanced around, searching for an outlet to plug in her charger. When the diner door banged, she jerked her attention to the new arrival. When the cop's eyes locked on hers, she grabbed her backpack and bolted down the short hall toward the restrooms.

Sheriff's Deputy Thomas Broussard covered the distance to the restrooms in three long strides, but the girl escaped through the back exit into the night.

The cook, a slob named Dwayne Givens, called after him. "Problem, Officer?"

Broussard paused outside the back door to scan the crumbling pavement and the dented dumpster at the lot's edge. Beyond the diner's lot were the deserted streets of Darkness Falls and blocks of derelict buildings to hide in. Broussard had no intention of searching for her. Not after dark. Not in Darkness Falls.

He stepped back inside. "Do you know that girl?"

Givens pushed a dirty rag around the table the kid had occupied. "Never seen her before."

"A trucker reported picking up a hitchhiker who insisted on being let out here. Why do you think that was?"

Givens heaved a beefy shoulder up and down. "No idea. She used the bathroom and ordered the meatloaf. She a runaway?"

"If you see her again, call the sheriff's office. Where is your useless town constable?"

"Melvin? He's at Vicky's Tavern, like every night."

"I figured Melvin more likely be at 'The Watering Hole.' That seems more his kind of dump. Anyway, call him. We need to talk."

Givens snorted. "He's been drinking since four. He ain't answering his calls."

Broussard clamped his jaw to stifle a shudder. He'd have to track down Melvin to report the runaway and then write up an account confirming he'd done his duty. But that meant spending upwards of thirty more minutes in Darkness Falls, something he wanted to avoid with every fiber of his being.

Running always made Charlotte feel better. On the nights she found her mom passed out on the sofa, Charlotte jogged to her neighbor's house to crash. When her stepdad lectured her about skipping school, she ran to her friend's house and smoked weed until she felt better. And when Justin told her he was sick of her drama and dumped her for a damn cheerleader, she ran clear out of town.

No cars followed Charlotte as she jogged down a street lined with dark shops, but she turned down a side street and then another, just in case. No cars moving on those streets, either. The cop hadn't followed, which surprised her because she just knew her stepdad probably reported her for stealing the eighty bucks from his wallet before she took off.

Convinced she'd lost the cop, Charlotte slowed to a walk but continued her zigzag path through the town. Many of the shop windows were boarded over and those that weren't were clouded with dust. With maybe one working street light per block, she couldn't tell if those shops were abandoned or just closed for the night. Either way, an empty shop was a decent place to crash, unless it had alarms or cameras. She didn't notice any but moved on anyway, enjoying the freedom of going where she wanted, when she wanted.

No one judged her when she was alone. Even on unfamiliar streets in the middle of nowhere, solitude was better than her mom's whiney clinging, Justin's betrayal, and her stepdad's criticism. Better to walk alone in a strange town than deal with all that negativity.

Charlotte tripped over a tree root pushing through a crack in the sidewalk. Cursing, she moved into a pool of yellow streetlight to check her shoelaces. She was proud of her new Converse high tops. She'd lifted them from an outlet store while waiting for her mom to buy another damn handbag. Charlotte had slid them into the shopping bag she was carrying and walked from the shoe store, cool as anything. Lifting stuff made her feel clever, like losing that cop at the diner did.

She wondered if the cop knew about her shoes or the denim jacket she'd snatched from her friend's closet. She'd never worn the jacket at home because somebody might recognize it, but she grabbed it when she left, free of the small-town busybodies.

Charlotte walked until the sidewalk ended, then continued along the asphalt road past wide lots with houses set well back from the street. The houses were one story, boxy, and looked as though they'd been built at the same time from the same plan. Some were lit up inside, but most weren't.

Spending the night in an empty house seemed like a better idea than an old store. There might be a bed and even a bathroom with running water. Charlotte slowed her walk until she found three unlit houses in a row. All three appeared abandoned, with sagging roofs and lawns full of dead weeds. An excited shiver ran through Charlotte, like when she was about to lift something. After scanning the street one last time, she made for the middle house.

Charlotte dashed through the barren lawn, then ducked behind a thorny shrub beside the squarish front porch. She squatted there until she guessed five minutes passed, then leaned out for a peek.

No porch lights popped on, and no cop car rounded the corner.

Charlotte counted to one hundred, then eased to her feet and peered through the streaky front window.

The curtain inside twitched.

She yelped and stumbled backward into the thorny bush. Unbalanced, the weight of her backpack dragged her to the ground. Charlotte pushed to her knees, ready to run, but no lights flipped on. The front door didn't burst open. No irate homeowner ordered her off the property.

It took a full minute for her heart to stop banging.

Charlotte concluded no lights didn't mean nobody was home, and the inn sounded like a better idea. She could spend the night at the Darkness Falls Inn, hitch a ride to the next town in the morning, and maybe find a job there. Having to find work was inevitable, but she'd hoped to be further away from home. Charlotte was unsure how far she'd traveled, but it wasn't far enough if cops were still chasing her.

After walking for maybe an hour, she still hadn't returned to town, which was puzzling because it had taken her only twenty minutes to get through the pathetic downtown and into the residential area. She must have lost track of the turns.

Charlotte pulled out her phone, hoping she had enough charge to open the map app. The screen's glow comforted her, but she had no signal, zero bars, and the battery sat at six percent. She shoved the phone into her jacket pocket and walked on.

The darkness was almost total now, the only light provided by a half-moon, its glow barely enough to see where the pavement ended and narrowed to a rutted dirt path. With each step, the trees grew thicker and pressed so close a branch brushed her arm.

She jerked away, pressing her arms to her chest. The sudden movement made her stumble, and the world seemed to shift sideways. Disoriented in the dark, Charlotte felt a whine accumulating in her and hated herself for being a scared little girly-girl. To keep from getting too wound up, she willed her feet onward. After a few steps, the trees parted, revealing a sight so unexpected, Charlotte froze on the spot.

The woods ended at an expanse of crumbling asphalt with a three-story building crouching at its center. The building's smokestacks stretched into the night sky, and tall windows on the top floor reflected moonlight. Charlotte felt drawn to those reassuring silver glints of light and walked on as the weak half-moon revealed a rundown parking lot filled with cars. Her spirits soared. Cars meant people.

Charlotte ran toward the parking lot but slowed as an ache rose in her knee. When she reached the vehicles, she strolled through the ranks, letting her fingers glide over the dull and rusting hulks. They were old-timey cars, like the ones at the vintage car shows her stepdad dragged her to, but not shiny, restored, custom jobs. These appeared to have been rusting in place since the late 1950s, maybe earlier. Charlotte hadn't paid attention to model years at the car shows.

A graveyard. She'd stumbled into an automobile graveyard.

Her hopes of rescue were toast unless the place had a night security guard. Charlotte turned her attention to the vast crumbling rectangle of a building. Peeling paint, once white, now a murky gray against the brick wall, declared it *The Darkness Falls Steelworks.*

Charlotte scanned the building's base for a lit office, guard shack, or even the bobbing flashlight of some poor underpaid sap making night rounds. Seeing no signs of light or life, she craned her neck to the windows glinting in the moonlight high above her head. White flashes bounced off the panes.

No, not flashes. They were evenly spaced dots, and the dots remained even as clouds engulfed the moon. The sparkling dots mesmerized her. As Charlotte studied them, ovals appeared around the dots. The ovals flattened, then tilted upward at the outside corners until each windowpane wore a set of silver-white eyes.

Charlotte blinked at them.

The eyes blinked back, then widened in a fierce glare.

Her dinner congealed in her gut, then rose, filling Charlotte's mouth with acid mush. She screeched and scurried through the ranks of derelict vehicles to the trees. One trembling backward glance confirmed the eyes were growing larger and brighter.

Quaking with fear, Charlotte ducked into the trees, but the demonic eyes followed. She howled another primal scream and staggered deeper into the woods.

Charlotte ran and didn't stop running until her breath came in shallow gasps and a cramp rose on her right side. Staggering to a halt, she vomited, then dropped to her knees, desperate for air. Her quivering lips formed the word Mom, but she made no sound.

After her breathing calmed, Charlotte considered her surroundings with hesitant darting glances. She was on a narrow, rutted path. It wasn't the same dirt road she'd followed from town, but at least the trees didn't press in so closely. Though the ghostly eyes no longer followed her, she was alone, lost, and more frightened than she'd been in her life.

He tried to warn you, "Kevin said you shouldn't stay here, but you had to…"

Charlotte pounded the ground with her fists. "Get it together, girl. You let a trick of the light scare the crap out of you. Nothing's chasing you. Find a place to sleep. Things will look better in the morning."

Damn, she sounded like her mom. For a drunk, Charlotte's mom was an abnormally positive thinker, always assuming the best about people. What could be dumber?

Charlotte laughed at herself, pushed to her feet, noticing her filthy, scuffed Converse high tops. *They'll clean up.* She spit, wiped her mouth clean on the sleeve of her grungy denim jacket and walked on.

She kept her mind off the steel mill by wondering how Justin took the news that she'd skipped town, leaving his sorry ass to drudge away in his dad's hardware store while dreaming of college. He might make it there unless he got Little Miss Cheerleader knocked up. Then it was back to the hardware store, an apartment over his parent's garage, debt, and divorce. Not for Charlotte. She'd escaped *that* merry-go-round, the one her mom rode with a rum and Coke in one hand and a remote in the other.

It had to be after midnight when the woods ended, revealing an expansive lawn surrounding an unnatural looking mansion. Charlotte shuddered with uncertain laughter, scared she was imagining it, but this was no trick of the light. Real lamps blazed in every window on three floors. A circular drive lined with cars led to a columned marble porch. At its center, imposing double doors flanked by arched windows beckoned her to safety.

Charlotte pressed her fingertips to her eyes, then let her hands drop to her sides. The house was still there, full of light. Jazzy music, singing, and laughter poured from within.

Moaning with relief, she strode past a row of cars from another era. Though older than the rusted hulks at the mill, these antiques were shiny, perfectly preserved.

Charlotte straightened her spine and fashioned a smile as she climbed the three steps leading to the tall doors. Under the comforting glow of electric light, she raised her hand to grasp the heavy brass knocker but withdrew. Her nails were long and grimy and she guessed she looked every bit the street rat, but she wanted inside, so she brushed the hair from her face, knocked, then quickly hid her hands behind her back.

The door swung inward, revealing a man with his back to her, talking to someone inside. He was tall and dressed in a fitted black suit, a tuxedo, maybe.

"Excuse me, mister. I'm lost. Can I use your phone?" Her voice sounded hollow and distant, muffled by the music and voices from the house.

The man turned and Charlotte's gaze dropped to his shoes, so shiny they reflected the porch light. She raised her head to the brilliant white shirt beneath the black jacket, then to his face.

It was all wrong. Leather-dry skin stretched over his bones and red eyes glowed from within lidless sockets.

The mummy-man bent forward in a shallow bow. "May I help you, young lady?" With each word, teeth clicked from within a lipless mouth dripping with dirt and gravel.

"Ah. Ah." Charlotte couldn't form words. She stumbled backward off the porch and landed on her butt, sending a jolt of pain down her spine. When the animated corpse stepped outside, Charlotte's legs churned to scoot away from the skeletal hand waving a cocktail glass at her.

"Come in, have a drink with us." The monster weaved and wavered on his feet, then lurched from the porch to the driveway.

Charlotte flipped to her knees and crawled until she regained her feet, then ran screaming into the night, chased by a taunting laugh that grew louder as it followed her through the forest.

She ran, her mind focused on one goal—escape.

Charlotte was aware of breaks in the trees and ramshackle buildings set in broad fields, but she didn't stop. Whiffs of manure and wood smoke rose and faded on a chill breeze. The silence grew so profound she might have been alone on the planet, except for distant rustling caused by animals or the wind. It didn't matter which. Charlotte ran.

Time ceased to exist. Charlotte wasn't aware of anything besides putting one foot in front of the other, her arms dangling at her sides, hands balled into fists. Her vision blurred and sometimes vanished altogether, but she didn't stop moving.

After she didn't know how long, Charlotte doubled over, gasping for breath. Her hair spilled over her shoulders as she bent forward, hands pressing on knobby knees.

When she raised her head, it was as if she'd awoken from a long nightmare. A morsel of reason returned, enough to appreciate that she'd made it back to town, though it wasn't a part she recognized from before. The sidewalks were planks lined with wooden rails, and the air smelled of straw. Streetlights on ornate poles flickered as though lit with candles. And the windows in this part of town weren't dusty or boarded up. On one shop window, fancy lettering spelled out *Darkness Falls Dry Goods and Sundries.*

Sundries. What the hell were sundries?

While bent over catching her breath, Charlotte studied her prized high-tops in the flickering light. The shoes weren't just dirty; they were in shreds. Her toes poked through the canvas, and the soles were worn through. The laces were broken, and every seam frayed or split.

Charlotte pressed up on aching knees. She could get new shoes. All that mattered now was the light. Dawn would come soon. People would fill the streets, and she'd be safe.

She shrugged her pack from her aching back, leaned against a lamppost, and frowned at the sliver of a moon above her. It had been a half-moon at the steelworks. Now it was a sliver. That couldn't be, not in one night.

A queasy fear gripped her as she recalled the thing at the mansion. Did it catch up with her? Attack her? Had she been knocked out, unconscious for days?

Distant footsteps heightened her dread.

Clop, clop, pause.

Charlotte held her breath.

Clop, clop, pause; closer now.

She released the breath and whimpered. Footsteps on wooden planks continued their purposeful stride. Was it him again, the mummy-man? Moments before, she'd hoped for company, the safety of a crowd, but the slow, deliberate nature of these steps squeezed the breath from her lungs.

She waited.

Clop, clop, pause, then a jingle like spurs on boots.

As Charlotte turned to run, a chill breeze caressed her right ear in an evil drawl. "Welcome to town, little miss. Make yourself right at home."

Charlotte pushed off the lamppost and escaped down the narrow alley between two wood-frame buildings. The passage seemed impossibly long, but the clop, clop of boots still reached her, so she kept running, breathing ragged, heart pounding.

The buildings blocked what little light the moon reflected. Plunged into a tunnel of darkness, Charlotte again lost track of time. She guessed an hour passed before the echo of the boots faded and a patch of light illuminated the mouth of the alley. When she stumbled into the moonlight, the horrifying town vanished behind her.

In a pool of soft light cast by a full moon, she spun, arms outstretched and hair flying around her. She'd finally escaped the darkness. Here, the air was clear, cold, and smelled of a hundred

Christmas trees. Darkness Falls was gone, and Charlotte felt free and safe.

Exhausted, she slid her back down the trunk of an ancient oak, closed her eyes, and dreamed of home.

～

Dawn filtered through Charlotte's eyelids, waking her. She moaned and twisted her face to escape the pink-gold light.

Her bursting bladder nudged her further along the road to wakefulness. She'd slept sitting upright, her butt on damp ground, her back against a rough cement wall. Squeezing her eyes tight against the dawn, she used the wall to help push to her feet.

Charlotte fumbled with the zipper of her jeans, but her fingers, bent into claws from the cold, refused to cooperate. She gave up and shoved her jeans over her hips, surprised at how easily they dropped to her feet.

Pressing her back against the wall again for support, she squatted and let her bladder empty. The warm flow felt good, and Charlotte turned her face to the sun, eyes shut against the glare.

She finished and patted the ground until her fingers touched the damp leather straps of her backpack. Charlotte dragged the pack close, then opened one eye to search for a tissue to clean herself.

As she poked her fingers into the outside pocket, she opened both eyes to examine pale brown spots on the back of her hand. She remembered falling in mud. God, she must be filthy, and she shrank from her own stink.

Her vision was fuzzy, so she brought the hand closer to her face. Her prized denim jacket's cuffs made her forget her dirty hands. The cuffs weren't just frayed. They were ripped, faded, and encrusted with layers of grime and mud that would never wash out.

What had happened to her? Had she been beaten? Did she have a concussion? *Is that why my vision's so blurry?*

Charlotte pitched forward to her knees, tried to stand, but couldn't get her balance. Bare-assed, on her hands and knees in a stream of her own urine, she cried in frustration. The tears distorted her vision, magnifying her splayed hands. A moan escaped her, and she rolled onto her side, rocking in time to her sobs.

Deputy Thomas Broussard entered the Darkness Falls Diner wishing he were anywhere else, but he couldn't face another sleepless night worrying about the kid.

He'd alerted the useless constable of an endangered minor in his town and put out an alert for the girl, but she hadn't been seen. Broussard couldn't fathom why this runaway's fate had kept him up. She was healthy, fast on her feet, and probably long gone.

No one would blame him for not chasing the girl into the darkness. Still, he'd feel better if he saw her safe, so he returned to Darkness Falls on his day off in civilian clothes, guessing she had run from the uniform the night before. He might get a word in before she took off this time.

The diner's door creaked on its hinges and slammed behind him like every time. Broussard scanned the dining room, but didn't see the girl. He approached Dwayne Givens, who leaned his elbows on the sticky yellow counter and watched the deputy's approach without a word.

"Did that runaway come back?" Broussard asked.

Givens pressed his lips together and shook his head. "Haven't seen her, but she'll likely stop in when she's hungry." He pushed back from the counter and wiped his hands on a stained towel.

"She didn't stay at the inn," Broussard said.

"Probably caught a lift out of town. You want to wait, see if she shows up?" Givens asked. "I'll make you some breakfast."

Broussard ignored him and strolled among the tables and booths. Most of the faces were familiar.

A dusty homeless man that everyone knew used both shaking hands to lift a coffee mug to his lips. The man shrank from Broussard as he passed.

In another booth, a shifty-eyed couple, both in jeans and red flannel shirts, followed his progress with expressions of frank hostility. The deputy couldn't recall their names, but wished them a good morning. They turned from his gaze.

Alone at a table by the window, Miss May-Ellen Dawes, the crazy old town historian, studied her bible over a pile of greasy hash browns. She ignored his nod as he passed.

A stranger hunched over a mug of Givens' vile coffee in the back booth near the restrooms. Matted white-gray tendrils hung to the bony shoulders of a woman wearing clothes so tattered it was impossible to envision what they'd looked like new. Even her shoes were in shreds.

Broussard was sure he'd never seen her in Darkness Falls or anywhere else and wondered how she'd gotten there. Concerned she'd been granny-dumped by a family member sick of caring for her, he strode across the diner for a closer look.

As with the wino, she clutched a coffee mug in trembling hands. Broussard stopped at her table and squatted so they'd be face-to-face.

The woman raised her head and struggled to focus on him.

Broussard spoke softly. "Mornin' ma'am. You doing okay today?'

Her liver-spotted, skeletal hand grasped his as she raised her face to him. Mud and grit filled deep wrinkles in her heart-shaped face, and startling blue-green eyes searched his.

"Please, mister." Her voice sounded ancient, dry as dust. "Can you give me a lift out of here?"

OUROBOROS

PAUL EAGLE

DANNI

I still have so many questions but now there is one thing I know for sure. I have to go to the old steel factory. Tonight. For revenge.

The factory has been abandoned for years, and it's now home to the Mallone brothers. They are the gang that runs most of this sorry excuse for a town. Most people go out of their way to avoid them, but I need some answers and I plan on getting them before my payback. Even if it means risking everything.

DETECTIVE SANCHEZ

I'm standing in this rotting dump of a junkyard looking over a woman who is probably in her mid-30's. At least that's the conclusion I've come to. The forensics team hasn't arrived yet, so I haven't actually touched the body. She is in bad shape. Real bad shape. Her ear is missing, there's a golf ball sized whole on the other side of her head and her face is little more than fleshy pulp. Both of her arms are zip-tied behind her back and are gruesomely misshapen and broken. Clothes shredded. I wish I could say that the sight of this made me queasy. I wish that I felt even a shred of the sickness that I used to feel back when I was a rookie. But five years in Darkness Falls, and this has become just another Tuesday on the job.

I still don't really know how I ended up here. Maybe it was because no one else wanted the job. Maybe it was because I was young and stupid. Maybe some part of me wanted to punish myself for my previous sins. The reason doesn't really matter. This is now my home – and I'm not a big fan of murder on my watch.

I take one last glance at the scene as the sun begins to rise. The girl has a recognizable gun tossed carelessly alongside her, and her cell phone lays shattered on the ground in front of her. I think for a second about taking the phone, but I decide against it and leave it for forensics. The rest of the team will be here any minute and will no doubt update me on what they find. Whoever did this must have really hated her. They obviously wanted her dead, but I can tell they wanted her to suffer too. And suffer she must have. They tortured her, killed her and dumped her here. A shiver runs through me as I brave the morning chill and begin my long walk back to town. The fog hovers low over what used to be the river, and even though the sun is coming up it remains dark and grey. It's always dark here, the kind of darkness that gets into your soul if you stay too long.

I have trouble shaking a weird feeling. I'm missing something. There was something very familiar about that girl. It gives me a sinking feeling deep in my stomach – though maybe I'm just hungry. I don't remember the last time I ate; or slept for that matter.

DANNI

It's dark by the time I get there. I'm shaking, though that could just be the cold. I pass through one of several holes in the metallic fence that outlines the perimeter of the factory. Once home to thousands of workers it now only contains ghosts, and memories of a more opti-mistic time. And the Mallone brothers of course.

The exterior floodlights haven't worked in decades, but a sliver of light emanating from under a door tells me that people are inside. Outside that main door is one of the Mallone's goons, smoking a cigarette. It's so dark that he can't see me, but I can't risk getting any closer. Not yet. I'm going to have to find another way in.

~

DETECTIVE SANCHEZ

Darkness falls is waking up. As I finally make it to the outskirts of downtown, I see graffiti-covered metal shutters being raised by shop-keepers who would rather be anywhere else than here. Piles of bundled up newspapers are being thrown off trucks, and litter empty doorways. The few people that pass me on the street don't even look up as they go about their day, bundled up in winter coats and scarves. Their eyes, like last night's trash, are stuck to the dirty sidewalk under-neath their feet.

I still haven't heard anything from my team, but that's not unusual. Most of the police force left Darkness Falls years ago. And one of them got killed in the line of duty. Those that physically remain have all but checked out mentally. We all still go through the motions and do what needs to be done, but never in a hurry. I'll swing by the station at some point later on and check in, but for now I need a cup of coffee and a quiet place to think.

~

DANNI

The loading doors to the factory floor are unattended. Security is almost non-existent as no one would dare mess with the Mallone's – no one in their right mind anyway. I pull the pistol out of my back pocket, my brother's gun, as I squeeze under the gap in the partially raised doors, being as careful as I can not to make any noise. This part of the factory is pitch black, and I can only just make out the edges of the shadowed and dilapidated machinery that takes up most of the factory space.

As I creep through the warehouse I begin to hear laughing and voices coming from the office in the back corner. My breath catches as I instinctively hug the wall and point the gun out in front of me. The door is only open a crack. It sounds like at least five people are inside but it might be a dozen. I don't really know what I expected to find here – but everything I came for is on the other side of that door.

DETECTIVE SANCHEZ

It's not even lunch time and I already need this day to be over. I can't even get a cup of coffee. I sat at a table, spent ten minutes in the café and was ignored the whole time. People really hate the cops in this town. To make things worse, I realize my phone is damaged. Taking it out of my pocket I notice that the screen is scratched to shit, and the thing won't even turn on. I don't remember how it happened. Probably last night. It's all still a blur. I must have tied a bigger one on at Vicky's than I had originally thought. Wouldn't be the first time. It explains the headache at least. I could say I did it in memory of my fallen officer but the truth is I just wanted to get drunk. And forget.

I decide that I needed to get to the Station. Hopefully forensics will be back, and the victim's phone will give me something that I can work with. I'll be able to get a shitty cup of coffee at the very least.

DANNI

Creeping closer to the office door I'm suddenly aware of a splitting pain in my head. I have no idea how long I've had this headache, but it's turning into a bad one and I'm finding it hard to think. I need to get my shit together. Quickly. Leaning against the wall I give myself a moment to take several long, drawn-out breaths as I try and force myself to relax. It doesn't work.

I continue onward toward the door slowly and deliberately. I can hear them much more clearly now. There is laughing and good-natured, though foul-mouthed teasing between the group, which mainly consists of insults directed towards various mothers. It's only now that I realise that I don't have anything that resembles a plan. I knew I had to come here and confront them. I was drawn here like some kind of magnetic attraction so strong it was inevitable. But now, standing directly outside, I don't know what to do next.

I could stay out here and listen in – see if their conversations offer up any insight. I could wait things out and see if any of the goons leave, then at least there'd be fewer people to worry about. Or I could ignore the outrage that's driven me here tonight against my better judgement, and just go home to bed.

Rather than overthink it, I check the gun, count to three, and burst through the door.

DETECTIVE SANCHEZ

It takes another hour to walk to the Station. I begin to feel foolish for not bringing my car this morning, but I'm in no real hurry to get anywhere today. The streets are deserted. No one lives in this part of the town anymore. The Darkness Falls Police Station is the only inhabited building in ten city blocks. Being that most of the town's occupants are less-than upstanding citizens, it is no real surprise that none of them choose to live around the only law enforcement presence in the area.

The main doors are wide open as I enter the building and take the stairs up to the third floor. I head straight for the kitchen. My headache is getting worse, probably from caffeine withdrawal. The kitchen is lifeless, and I am horrified when I see an empty coffee pot. It is the end of civilized society when the person that finishes the coffee doesn't bother to refill it. It should be a criminal offence. I feel the rage building in me, and I burst back out into the office ready to yell at the first person I see – but I don't see anyone. The whole floor is silent and empty. Where is everyone? I go back down the stairs to the second floor and find the same there. I even go down to the holding cells and drunk tanks only to find them empty too. What the fuck is going on? Has everyone abandon their post because one cop was murdered. Or had Darkness Falls gotten to all of them?

DANNI

Alfie and Harry Mallone are sitting around a table with a few other guys. They are huge. This is the first time I have seen them in person, and they certainly live up to their reputation. They are identical in almost every way, from their short blonde hair to their piercing blue eyes. They barely have a neck between them, as both of their heads are perched atop their wide and veiny shoulders. Both of their chests are close to bulging out of their matching grey tanks. I've been told that the only way to tell them apart is by their scars and tattoos, which differ slightly from brother to brother – but it makes no difference to me which is which. I want them both dead.

I point the gun at one of them, and immediately the three goons at the table jump to their feet and draw guns of their own, but Harry (or Alfie) waves them away with a lazy gesture of his sausage-fingered hand. The three guys leave the room through a side door and only the brothers, still seated, remain. The complete lack of fear is disarming. It's like they believe that even bullets cannot harm them. Looking at the sheer size and strength of their bodies I begin to have doubts myself.

Alfie (or Harry) nods to one of the vacant seats and shakily I sit, keeping the gun trained on Harry (or Alfie). He begins to pour whiskey in an empty glass from a nearby bottle. "We've been expecting you, Danni" he begins, voice thick as gravel, as he slides the glass over to me. "Drink up." he continues with a smile as his brother pulls a set of zip-ties out of his pocket. "You'll need it."

After that everything went dark.

~

DETECTIVE SANCHEZ

With no one to confer with I head back to Vicky's. No one even acknowledges my existence here as I take a seat at my usual booth. I used to at least receive a concerned glance or two from some of the patrons as I walked into the local bar, but today I get nothing. No one even hits on me, which might be the first time ever. It's a strange feeling, and I find myself almost longing for a snide comment or slur at my expense. I've got a lot of pent-up energy and wouldn't mind burning some of it off by taking some punk down.

This whole thing has got me rattled, and I never get rattled. It's a feeling that I hate, and I feel like the quicker I can figure this whole thing out, the quicker I can move on. I wouldn't mind getting some sleep.

Thinking back to this morning, I run the scene again in my head. She had a gun. Now that I think about it, it looked like a standard police issue. Where did she get it from? There's no way the murderer would bother planting it on her. That probably means that she knew what she was getting herself into, and she was clearly into some serious shit. And when I say murderer I mean murderers because the killing has all the earmarks of the Malone brothers.

I look up to see Vicky behind the bar glancing in my general direction. I raise my hand to try and get her attention, but she pretty much looks right through me before turning and serving someone at the bar. Fuck this day. The same thing happened at the café when I tried to get coffee.

The other thing that I still can't get my head around is how the victim looked so familiar, even though there wasn't much of a body left to look at. What was it about her build, her body that makes me think that I know who she was? Someone I met. I don't know anyone in town that fits the description. In fact, the person closest to her age, height and build would be....

And then it hits me all at once, like a freight train to the gut. The gun, the phone, the girl. Shit. My head spins and the ringing in my ears drowns out all of the background noise of the bar. Shit, Shit, Shit.

I still have so many questions but now there is one thing I know for sure. I have to go to the old steel factory. Tonight. For revenge.

Aurora Reborn

ELAINE GILMARTIN

She hated him so much, the smell of him, the sound of his voice, the way he chewed his food. His mere presence in a room drew a dark cloud over her, threatening to smother her in a haze of bitter tears.

And yet she stayed, and stayed, the reasons as empty and meaningless as his professions of love after the fact.

He probably wouldn't wake. A marching band, a parade of elephants, a crash of rhinos, and still Peter wouldn't wake.

Climbing to the back of the closet, the rising sun's illumination barely touching its recesses, she winced in pain, but covered her mouth when her knee connected with one of her high heels, as useless as the dresses hanging above. Her groping hands finally found it, the strap to her faded North Face backpack buried beneath a mass of sweaters, old college textbooks abandoned just like the degree they pretended to represent, and she pulled and pulled.

With its comforting weight in her arms, she scooched back on her butt, rose wobbly to her feet without the benefit of her hands, and craned her neck around the open closet door. She needn't have worried as the rise and fall of his bare chest in symphony with the wheeze of air through his nose told her all she needed to know.

Deaf and half-blind, Robbie, his hound dog, didn't stir either on his bed just under the window, face scrunched in doggie dreams, and although she loved and cared for him more, he was Peter's dog after all. She slipped into her Skechers, casting Robbie one final glance as she turned to the door and began the first steps on the long journey of grief.

Dark was the hallway, but she knew it well, and emerging into the living room, she spied her jacket on the couch where she threw it last night all to get to the bedroom first and lock the door behind her. Not fast enough.

Out on the front path, the cold sting of late November hit her and she cursed each leaf she stepped on as if they were sirens betraying her escape. Once in her Camry, she tossed her backpack on the passenger seat and pulled on her jacket, digging for the keys in the pocket. Turning the ignition, she regarded the small A-frame house emotionlessly, its faded yellow paint a testament to the death of hope and out of the driveway she tore.

No music, the phone still silenced, and she drove that way for some time savoring the quiet empty road and her command of it. Trees illuminated beautifully in gold and orange and red leaves formed a canopy over her and beckoned her onward wherever the road may lead.

Reality encroached only when she saw the sign for Dunkin at the entrance for the highway, her craving for caffeine suddenly ignited. A pick-up truck ahead of her on the drive-thru gave her a moment to take stock of what she had. Debit card, joint account, useless. Wad of cash saved from two years of waitressing, tips shrinking from their account, fattening the bag in which it was stuffed, amounting to nearly three thousand dollars at last count about a month ago. Wallet held a five, a ten, and a bunch of singles. She pulled out the five, ordered her coffee black, and accepted the change wordlessly.

Pulling to the side, she checked her phone. Half charged, no texts. 7 AM. Peter's hangovers often lasted near noon when they were bad. She had time. Heading west, as far west as geographically possible. California, an old high school friend in Venice Beach, open invitation. James. She hoped he still had a thing for her.

Opening the compartment under her arm, she felt for the phone charger so she could set it for directions. An empty, crumpled box of cigarettes and a ketchup-stained McDonald's napkin were all that greeted her hand. Peter. She hated how he thought he could just take her car, among other things.

Glove compartment, no. Under the seat, feeling around, glancing at the back seat. Nope, bastard took it again because he kept losing his own. Never mind, she thought, keep driving due west through Pennsylvania until the state line of Ohio and then worry about finding a Best Buy or something. She wanted as much distance between herself and Peter.

Karma Police on the radio, window open slightly, the air like fingers through her hair simultaneously lifting and pressing it against her face, and on she drove. The hours went by, the sun flirting at the edges of the clouds until hunger sent her off an exit. No drive-thru, so she entered the Wendy's restaurant, found the bathroom, and avoided looking at her reflection as she washed her hands, a flickering fluorescent light overhead.

Back in the car, she ripped off the straw paper with her teeth, unwrapped the chicken sandwich on her lap, and ate, stoically watching happy families in the parking lot, kids skipping to the restaurant holding a parent's hand. Sated, she finally dared to scroll through her phone and was not especially pleased to see the number of texts, each with a similar, and yet increasingly hostile, theme.

You at work?

*Where the **** are you?*

???

Won't get too far... followed by additional profanities.

Something about that last text disturbed her, the others of a more generic-nasty variety, that last...

Squishing the wrappers into a ball and tossing it to the back seat, she knew she had to be more purposeful with her movements. It would be dark in several hours, courtesy of daylight savings, and she would need rest. Opening her backpack, she dug below the stuff she packed when this quick-escape idea first came to her a few months ago, socks, leggings, a sweater, couple of t-shirts, finding the drawstring jewelry bag that ironically once held a bracelet Peter had given her for her birthday, now seemingly light-years ago.

Interestingly it was not tied bunny-ear style as was her habit and so when she drew the strings apart and pulled out a handful of Monopoly money, the shock she would have felt was already dulled.

He had found it, somehow found it and carefully replaced the old sweaters and textbooks as if it hadn't been disturbed, taking her meticulously saved, $2,838 and replacing it with apparent malicious glee with board game cash.

This left her with a commanding two dollars and change and a now-useless debit card. He likely contacted the bank already to freeze their account, an account she wouldn't have wanted to tap into anyway as it would broadcast her location.

Gas getting low. No phone charger. Abby? Her sister was a classic borderline; catch her on a good day and she would move heaven and earth to help, a bad and she would alert Peter and tell her she had it coming. Okay, no heads-up. She would simply show up on Abby's doorstep in the morning and appeal to her better nature.

So a detour then to Galla County, Ohio. She would have to use her phone for directions, saw she would cross West Virginia, then turned it off to conserve the charge and off she went, heart racing, hands gripping the steering wheel.

Had she ever loved him? She thought maybe once, couldn't feel it now of course. What he professed as love was control, what she returned was not love, but fear. He had cheated on her, blamed it on her for being *unavailable* after an appendectomy. He siphoned gas a few times from a neighbor when he was in between construction jobs, but Peter called himself a Christian and he was after all a man and so that made him good and right in his mind.

So likely no, since what he professed as love was control, what she returned was not love, but fear. That was not who she was, who she was she would reclaim.

Driving and driving with the sun sinking behind the West Virginia mountains, the canopy of trees no longer beautiful but menacing, she began to feel the full weight of her predicament, her bone-deep fatigue, her anger.

Gaslight on. Two dollars and change. When had she last seen an exit? Had she seen any since traveling down this route?

Then like an exclamation point to her question, a green reflective sign, small and askew, but a sign indicating a destination nonetheless, its arrow underlining the printed words, *Darkness Falls*.

A hint of a smile came to the corner of her mouth. *How appropriate.*

Exiting, the turn was much sharper than she anticipated, the Camry nearly coming to glide on one side. Correcting, her right front tire hit a stump with a pop, and then overcorrecting, she nearly drove into a big evergreen, corrected again with a tire squeal just missing a critter of some kind in the road, its tail disappearing into the thickening fog.

Coming to a stop at the end of what should be named suicide loop, she laughed nervously, *picked a bad time to give up smoking!*

Putting the car into park, she stepped out into the cool mist and surrounded as she was by a thicket of trees, glanced around for said critter before looking at her tire with dismay.

Flat.

In the fading light, she saw another sign, smaller, even more askew, but undeniably indicated Darkness Falls to the right, the darker of the ways, naturally.

Mindful of her dwindling gas reserves, she jumped back into the car and took her phone off airplane mode and typed to an acquaintance far away.

Still open to a guest?

Not anticipating an immediate response, she put the car into drive, moving at a snail's , the tire flopping, when she heard the ding.

Of course.

Smiling for the first time in hours, days, years, she could almost feel the warmth and sun and ocean spray across her face, a new start, an old friend, a light at the end of a tunnel she had long since entered.

So lost in her reverie was she that she hadn't noticed she was entering town-or what used to be a town. Desolate, she passed a coffee shop with its door boarded shut, a Smiley's Hardware & Feed! an old consignment shop with a doll's lifeless eyes peering at her from the storefront window. The sidewalk had grass sprouting up through its cracked and uneven surface, an old Chevy sat rusted in its death throes by a long since faded stop sign.

Great, she thought sarcastically, *wasted my gas and a tire for this?*

On she drove, recognizing the suicide loop from which she came would likely take longer to return than to find the one exiting the town.

Her Camry limped along, the gaslight on the dashboard mocking her. Out of habit, she slowed as she came upon a yield sign perched precariously at a traffic circle. *Guess I have the right of way,* she thought ridiculously and as she pressed gently on the accelerator, she did a sudden double-take.

Across the way, an ancient gas station, its pumps beneath a rain cover, a man leaning against one, a cigarette in the corner of his mouth, watching her.

So taken back was she, she simply sat and stared in return, thinking his motionless form was possibly a mirage until he raised a hand in apparent greeting.

Well, that's an invitation!

Rolling through the traffic circle, she pulled into the station, thankful there was sufficient light in the foggy gloom to reveal a man's scrawny frame, hair long and graying, and as she drove closer, his near-toothless smile seemed almost predatory, until she came to a stop. Smiling more broadly, he raised his hand again and tossed his cigarette, approaching in a manner more disarming.

She lowered her window, caution thrown to the wind, Peter having raised the bar in terms of what she deemed threatening.

"You are a breath of fresh air!"

He laughed, the odor of nicotine, rot, decay momentarily erasing her smile.

"Can't say I been told that before."

Uncomfortable yet desperate, "Um, gas?"

He laughed again, gesturing behind himself while she took in his filthy denim jacket, last washed when...?

"Ayup, but looks like you got bigger problems."

She laughed stupidly. "Tire, I know, exit caught me off-guard."

"Does everybody."

She hesitated again. "Um, I don't have cash, but I think my debit card still works," she said honestly. She had to get the hell out of here. If the card still worked, she would think it funny if Peter tried to follow her here. Enjoy *Darkness Falls*, bastard!

Stepping back, he waved his hand motioning for her to pull up to the pump. Doing so, she turned off the ignition and stepped out of the car looking around to see if there were any other signs of life or if this were simply a bizarre and unfortunate mirage.

Following her gaze, he pointed somewhere to the west. "There be a sandwich shop bout a half-mile down the road, but prolly closed already. You got the Travel'inn just beyond, Mara could fix you up with a room if you be wantin' some rest."

Facing him and making every effort not to recoil from his halitosis, "No, need to keep going, just hoping something can be done with the tire."

The man, who appeared to be anywhere from an old-looking forty to a young eighty, stepped away and looked at the tire scratching his receding hairline with a long yellowed fingernail.

"Ayup. Gotta figure if a patch'll do. Why'nt you get yourself a little refreshed and I'll do what I gotta do. And keep your card. We settle at the end," he said with a wink.

She smiled stupidly again, unsure what that meant, afraid he may change all four tires and the transmission just to shake her down.

Nodding, she reached back into her car and grabbed her backpack, and pointing with some apprehension asked, "Thataway?"

Nodding vigorously, he asked her name.

"My name? Dawn."

"Dawn? Oh, we have no dawns here."

Okay, she thought oddly, supposing these small-town people likely did indeed know the name of each of its residents. "Okay, then back soon," she said as breezily as she could muster.

Walking felt good. Muscles stiff from hours of driving, she savored the motion, but the air felt different, not the fresh mountain, pine-y scent she would have anticipated, instead stale, claustrophobic.

As if it had always been there, ahead the grayish outline of several low buildings, the sound of a truck rumbling somewhere in the distance, a horn, yet still nothing substantial.

She hated him, hated him, hated him more and more with each step. *He's why I'm here, he's why I have a crappy dead-end job, he's why I let my friends go, he's why I'm in this town that smells like death.*

She just had to get to James in Venice Beach. He would make things right, she would be happy again. Just get some water, directions, some luck with her card, the car.

A blur in her vision, dark and fast. Cat? Raccoon? Something else? Stopping, she looked up and in the mist she could make out the faded wood sign on the first low building, the Travel'inn, the letters in cursive followed by a cartoon palm tree and winking sun. Someone has a sense of humor.

Walking up the three wooden steps to the porch, she hesitated, feeling eyes on her. Turning, there were two figures in silhouette across the street, stock still, likely amazed anyone would stop here of her own volition.

Taking the final step, she advanced nervously to the door, debating whether to use the knocker given the absence of a doorbell or simply to walk inside, then opted for the latter.

An anachronism within an anachronism, she entered a large foyer, its rug well-worn and filthy, and saw decor from the early 1920s; an old-time radio, a phonograph propped up on the end of a long bar, behind it a mirror faded and cracked, beneath it bottles of alcohol. Swiveling her head, she saw on the wall to her left a community bulletin board, the most recent date she could discern was 1972 for a church potluck dinner, *venison stew welcome!*

To her right a movie poster for Elvis in *Jailhouse Rock*, concert posters for Jimi Hendrix, Jim Morrison, and oddly enough, Amy Winehouse. Straight ahead was an archway with elaborate oak molding, leading to a darkened hallway beyond. Above the arch was a dusty neon sign attributed to Jimmy Buffett, "*I'd rather die while I'm living than live while I'm dead,"* a sentiment that sat uneasily with her.

Sweeping through this as if an apparition, a woman in a long, mud-colored skirt and crocheted white sweater approached, a smile touching both corners of her mouth.

"I'm sorry, dear, have you been waiting long?" she sang, coming uncomfortably close with arms spread as if to embrace her.

Taking an involuntary step back, she stammered, "No, no, sorry, I...I was only hoping to get some water bottles for my trip."

Smile faltering, arms dropping, "Trip? Why, you've just arrived!"

As if anyone could think this place a desirable destination, she did not know, but she supposed given this was the woman's business, she couldn't fault her attempts to drum up business.

"I'm just waiting for my tire to be fixed, back at the, um, station down the road. Just the water. I'm actually in a real hurry. "

Nodding sympathetically, "Ironic how so many people are and yet it never changes the destination."

Raising an eyebrow quizzically, she regarded the woman, shoulder-length white hair, a cherubic, not unfriendly face, icy-blue eyes gleaming at her. "I suppose..."

Taking her arm, she sang, "No Bottled water but come sit and I will prepare you some tea."

"Oh, please don't trouble yourself! Tap water is fine," although she regretted that the moment she said it. What would she be drinking? Rust, mud, detritus?

Ushering her to a bar stool, the woman swooped around the bar, clinking glasses and running the tap. Depositing her backpack on the bar, she remembered she had no cash, so tap water it was, though the tea sounded wonderful. Taking in more of the decor, she noticed above the mirror several dead animal heads, a deer, a large rodent-looking thing, and most unsettling, a dog.

Following her gaze, the woman said, "My dog, Robbie. He was my favorite. Lived to be almost fifty, I had to honor him."

Assuming she meant dog-years, she nodded wordlessly, disturbed by the coincidence in name, and accepted the water glass, making every effort not to analyze it for little floating debris.

Extending her hand over the bar, she said, "I am Mara, and you?"

Swallowing and making every effort not to grimace, "Dawn."

The woman withdrew her hand. "Oh, we have no dawns here."

Apparently Mara and the toothless wonder shared the same sense of humor. Increasingly uncomfortable, especially with Robbie the unfortunately-named ancient hound staring down at her, she gulped the glass dry. "Well, thank you for the water, but I think I might walk back to see about my car before it gets dark."

"You don't have to leave, you know," Mara said rather stoically.

"But I do," she said slowly getting up.

Her face animated, Mara laughed a bit. "All I mean to say is that you have hours ahead of you to reach any decent town. I would imagine a good night's rest would be in order. We have our share of passersby and a good many find they never want to leave."

Dawn didn't know if that was comforting or not. Resisting the impulse to roll her eyes, she went on, "I'm actually heading west to meet up with a friend who offered to let me stay a bit, get back on my feet."

"And what has you off your feet?"

Taken aback, she gripped the bar with both hands. So accustomed was she not to share anything, not with her coworkers, her borderline sister, her narcissistic mom, anyone, that the idea of opening up to this strange woman was initially shocking, but then somehow...liberating.

"My boyfriend, well, see," she began, and sinking back onto the barstool, continued, "We met in college, he dropped out beginning of sophomore year, got work in construction, and then he made me drop out end of that year."

"Made you, huh?" she asked, head resting on one fisted hand.

"Well, he said we needed money for a place, neither of us has any good family, we were all on our own, you know, and so I did, but things just got worse over the years. I think we just ended up blaming each other for being nowhere."

"But it got worse, didn't it?" head still on her fist, icy-blue eyes locked onto hers.

She nodded, beginning to feel tears well in the corner of her eyes. She honestly didn't think she could cry anymore, so hardened had she become. It was as if her heart had turned to stone and all she knew was anger eating her away on the inside.

Mara patted her hand knowingly. "It's okay, dear. You are in a safe place. You would always be safe here. I think you need to stay. No more running or hiding or lying or sneaking. Wouldn't that be...liberating?"

Liberating, odd her choice of word. For a moment, she could see it in her mind's eye, small town, same familiar faces, no fear, no stress, no choices to be made. She could sleep as deeply as she wanted, no more being on edge with one eye open expecting a slap, a threat...just sleep and know finally what it was to be at peace...

Dawn was on the verge of saying 'Yes, I'll stay here forever' when her eyes traced up to the face of the stuffed dog. A chill went through her as if shaking herself out of a bad dream. She saw something else in this woman's eyes, a gleam, not one of commiseration and empathy, but...*hunger*?

Pulling her hand away as if she'd touched a snake, she said, "I'm taking too much of your time...I..I really should go."

"And yet you don't seem sure, dear. You know you've always been able to choose, right? The weight of it can be very frightening."

Frozen, she stared back as Mara swept one arm to the right, indicating the arch and the hallway beyond. She followed the gesture with her gaze, seeing more than a long, dark hallway. Shapes, moving, a low murmur, not unpleasant, and yet...

Coming back to herself, she jumped back up. "I would pay you, but...um, my boyfriend...he found the money I've been stashing...he took it all and he..." tittering nervously... "he replaced it with Monopoly money...can you believe, well, he has this mean streak."

Dawn was backing up towards the door.

"And yet you chose to stay...?"

"It's not that simple," she intoned defensively.

"Nothing is and yet at the same time, is as simple as pie." Mara came around the bar, and she felt inertia take hold as it had at so many points in her life as if she never knew hard ground but rather quicksand, feet stuck, powerless to extricate herself, and now with this odd woman coming towards her, somehow both comforting and menacing at the same time and just like with Peter, she stood and stood and stood and never knew why. Rooted in her indecision.

Clutching her backpack to her chest, she watched wordlessly as Mara came to stand within inches of her face, sweeping both arms out this time, one towards the archway, the other toward the door.

"Sometimes we see what we want to see and sometimes what we want to see is the prison of our own making."

Eyes locked on the woman's icy-blues, it felt like it would never break until the sound of a car rumbled out in front of the Travel'inn, a familiar sound, one that broke her reverie, and without another glance beyond the archway, she bolted for the exit, down the steps to her waiting Camry, running, keys in the ignition, the cantankerous mechanic standing at the open door, cigarette in his hand. Dawn jumped in, sped away.

Shaking almost violently, she turned for a quick glance in the back seat, convinced toothless would have jumped in demanding to *settle at the end,* or Mara would be there beckoning her to *stay a while.* But she saw only her old Wendy's wrapper. On the passenger side her back-pack had opened when she tossed it in and lying on the seat was the old jewelry bag that once held a gift given in what may have been love, but now held real dollars crammed unceremoniously into it. 2,838 of them.

Tearing around the sharp turn, this time without clipping the tire, Dawn was determined not to glance back at the Travel'inn, nor the gas station and all the other buildings looming in the fog. Or the remnants of Darkness Falls. No, she was too busy seeing something quite different in her mind's eye, a beautiful beach, endless sand glittering like jewels slipping away into the ocean waves, and she–alone, wonderfully, blessedly alone. That was her choice.

Her decision.

DELIBERATE DESCENT TO DARKNESS FALLS

BETHANI BRIANNA

"What brings you to Outer Pass?" The bartender lazily swiped at the counter before setting a gin and tonic in front of Josh. There was a good old-fashioned beer for Hansen next to him. "Seems people who come to this place is either running from the law or they IS the law, tryin' to catch up," she said.

Josh grinned. "I guess we're more of the rule-breaking guild. Nothing any lawmen are interested in chasing at this point, but we'll keep you posted." He winked and Hansen rolled his eyes.

Josh was a hopeless flirt. Hansen thought it was more a skill he had inadvertently developed than any indication of where his romantic interests lay. He would flirt with a beautiful young maiden and her grandmother at the same time. But most of the women seemed flattered by it, which could be very useful in their rather unorthodox existence. Mary the bartender was his latest focus.

Josh and Hansen were inseparable friends and went way back to grade school. Even then, when their peers were dreaming of becoming firemen or astronauts or doctors, they were uniquely agreed that all of the careers mentioned seemed tedious, dull and ultimately somewhat enslaving. It was in high school when they discovered videography. They could film whatever they wanted, whenever they felt like it and as long as they kept it interesting they could have complete creative control and make a pretty decent living as well.

Currently they were working on a docuseries called Local Haunts. They traveled around, listening to local legends and ghost stories, visiting the place the stories originated and giving their audience exactly the mixture of information and intrigue they desired. The trick with things like this was to leave some questions unanswered, but to give enough information for them to try to puzzle out different possibilities for themselves. People ate it up. Everyone wants to be a sleuth.

Josh and the bartender had been amicably chatting while Hansen was busy typing on his cell. Josh's charms seemed to be working because the woman's face was flushed and her eyes bright.

"So really- what brings you to town? How long are you staying?" Mary asked.

"Not long, I'm afraid. We're what you might call investigative journalists. We're here about an old abandoned place called Darkness Falls. From what we hear, this is the last bit of civilization before we reach our destination."

The bartender had stopped smiling and her face had gone pale. "Don't go there," she said.

Hansen stopped in mid-type and gazed up at her. Josh raised his eyebrows and quirked his mouth into a half smile. "Don't you fret, Mary. We'll only stay a day or so, then we'll be passing through again on our way back. Maybe we'll even stay for a bit before heading out. Tell you about our adventures."

Mary shook her head. "If you go to Darkness Falls, you won't be coming back. Least not the same way you went in. The darkness doesn't let people leave. Not with their minds intact anyway."

"I've heard the story," Josh agreed, that silly smile still on his face. "Beautiful land of plenty. Crashing waterfalls, winding river. Friendly people. Everything perfect so long as it was just the farmers and their chapel. Then the steel factory moved in, polluting the land and increasing the population." He shrugged disarmingly. "Sounds like a story made up by people afraid of urbanization."

Mary looked unimpressed by Josh's flippancy. "You didn't hear the half of it. I could tell you stories...people don't go there. Not on purpose. Except for fools," she said, looking at them severely. "There's evil there that lives on there. That doesn't sleep. You see, the Falls didn't vanish. That's what you heard, isn't it? The Falls dried up and the river with them, leaving a barren desert? But they didn't vanish... they went dark. They're still there, changed. Now they feed the evil, give it power." She paused and poured the men another drink, and discreetly slugged a shot from under the bar.

"You want proof? There was a man used to live here. Don't know his given name. I reckon he had one, but folks round here just called him Jay. Everybody loved Jay. The type of guy who would give you his coat in a snowstorm, even if it meant he'd freeze. But as he got up in years his mind started to go. I reckon nowadays they call it dementia. He started wandering. He didn't have any next of kin-not that anybody knew about. But people 'round here loved him so, they divided the responsibility of looking after him amongst themselves. It worked pretty well too-up until old Mr Lemon was taking his shift. Mr. Lemon lived 'bout a mile down the way from Jay and that night he was taking care of Jay he saw a mighty blaze the likes of which he'd never seen afore. Rushed right on home to find his barn burning.

"They never did find out the cause of the fire, but by the time things settled down enough for people to start asking about Jay, he was gone. They sent out a search party and they combed these mountains. Every-where except Darkness Falls of course. But the more time that passed, the more convinced folks became that that had to be where he'd gone."

Josh smiled. "That does make for the best story, doesn't it? But just for logic's sake, these hills are pretty vast. You can't tell me that they searched every hill, every crevice between every rock..."

"I wasn't finished," Mary replied coolly. "People gave up looking after a few months, went back to business as usual. And then the chil-dren started complaining of nightmares. Hearing voices, moans, screams. From the west." She looked at them significantly. "You know Darkness Falls lies not more'n fifty miles west of here? Less'n that as the crow flies."

She seemed to be waiting for some kind of response, but Josh just sat there with an indulgent smile on his face.

"Weird," Hansen said, mostly just to have something to fill the empty space. He wasn't a people person like Josh. Social situations were awkward for him and small talk excruciating. He used exactly the words he needed to get the job done and no more. It worked. Mary continued on with her tale.

"Well, some months after Jay disappeared, he comes stumbling into town. From the west," she added, looking pointedly at Josh. He raised his hands in an "I surrender" gesture, that stupid smile still playing about his lips.

"Half his right arm was missing. He could barely walk. His skin had an awful green tinge to it and his mind was completely gone. Ever since he walked into town the children started falling ill. Every single one under thirteen years. He was like a rabid dog, foaming at the mouth. Attacked three people, bitin' and clawin'. The worst of it though was those eyes. If you looked at 'em same time as they was lookin' at you, you was blind within the hour.

"Sheriff had to chain him up in an old shack just outside of town just to keep people safe. His howlin' filled the streets for three days before it stopped, quite sudden after the sheriff had been out there to give him a plate of food. But that silence...it was eerie-like. Next day the deputy went down to check it out. There were the chains, the plate of food, untouched. But old Jay-he was gone. And so was the sheriff."

"That's a downright chilling tale. Hope your grandma didn't use it as a bedtime story," Josh said, signaling for another drink, hoping to lighten the mood, make her smile.

Hansen grunted, reading something in Mary that Josh appeared to have missed. She wasn't joking and she wasn't amused.

She slapped the towel down in front of them and grabbed their glasses, dumping their unfinished liquor down the sink. "Bar's closed, Gents. You can't say I didn't try to save your lives."

In a matter of moments Josh and Hansen found themselves standing outside with a crowd of disgruntled patrons.

"I don't think that was the usual closing time," Josh remarked, scratching his chin.

Hansen glanced sidelong at Josh. "Nice to know you're capable of striking out."

He was about to come back with a retort when a gravelly voice came from behind them.

"Arrogant twit."

Josh whirled around. "Excuse me?"

The guy was frail and wizened under a frayed ball cap. A loose dress shirt hung over a pair of worn jeans and he was the width of a flagpole. "You heard me. You come all the way out here, think you're gonna make a name for yourself covering Darkness Falls? Think your separation from it makes you wiser'n the people who live here?"

"Not at all," Josh began.

"Save it. I can see you're a man used to gettin' what he wants but I'll tell you right now, what works for you out there in yonder world- it ain't gonna work for you in Outer Pass. And sure as hell not in Darkness Falls."

Something in the man's words seemed to strike Josh. His breath was ladened with liquor but it was like the syllables were sinking in and doing some work behind the scenes. Hansen watched as all the polish and veneer fell away from his friend. Josh opened his mouth, then shut it again and merely stared at the man.

The man raised his eyebrows in what might have been approval, but didn't comment on it. "That little story Mary told you, Jay and the Sheriff vanishing...that happened last Saturday. Mary's little niece, Lila- she's one of them that fell ill."

Hansen's mouth went dry. Last weekend? This hadn't had time to grow into a tall tale or a legend. This was an experience... a memory they were still living. This town that they had so off-handedly agreed to examine, it could be the real deal and not one of those stories they had to puff up to sound scary.

"If you're looking for the switch that started it all...well that one does stretch back in time, long before living memory. But that doesn't make it any less true."

He peered at them inquisitively, then looked at Hansen's camera bag. "You do some type of Yubetoo or TubeYou or something?"

Hansen bristled, caught between being insulted and amused, but Josh, having recovered from his earlier speechlessness, smoothly cut in.

"Something like that. We're videographers. We sell our stuff a little higher up the line...television channels, streaming services..." he trailed off as he realized the old man wasn't even trying to follow.

"Look, I own that there Inn 'cross the street there. Name's O'Reilly. Sean O'Reilly. Definitely Irish, though I've never been to Ireland meself." He shrugged. "Why don't I hook you up with a room. There's a cafe in the lobby. I can tell you the story. You can even run that camera, use it in the bit you're doing."

Josh and Hansen looked at each other. "Well, sounds good to me."

They were settled in the lobby ten minutes later, with wall paper and glass enclosed breakfronts right out of a Rockwell painting, when O'Reilly began.

"A long, long time ago, back so far no one can rightly recollect the year, that little town you know as Darkness Falls was originally called Light Falls. And bring light they did, those pristine waters. T'were a magical place. Only three families it were that started the place, but even as the place steadily grew, Light Falls maintained its reputation for beauty, peace and contentment. It was paradise, a real heaven on earth.

"It was never about the number of people who came, that weren't what destroyed Light Falls. It was WHO came. Helen Finn. That's where she met up with Dezi Lars.

"Helen Finn was an outsider. When she came strolling in she was a young adult. Had never known a day's love in her life. She learned how to look after herself and like so many in that situation, that meant lying and stealing and hurtin' others if she needed.

"Dezi was one of Light Falls' own. Came from one of the first three families in fact. But there was something off about the girl from the start. Born without a conscious, she were. No empathy, no compassion. Still, she was a smart girl. When her elders told her she had to stop doing certain things in order to be accepted by society, she did. She took to drawing out her depravities instead. People thought that a safe enough alternative and so it was. Til Helen came.

"Helen and Dezi bonded instantly as the outcasts, girls who didn't quite fit the mold expected of them. I doubt either one would have become what they did without the other. But the day they met... that was the beginning of the end.

"Helen brought with her an ancient book of spells. No one knows where she got it but the rumor is, the second it crossed the border the light from the Falls started to dim. The girls started to experiment with the spells, Helen using her forceful voice, Dezi contributing her drawings to the pages. They made it their own. Whether they meant to or not, when they spoke the incantations they were drawing upon the power of the Falls, tainting them just a little with each spell. Wickedness will do that- seep in slowly and poison the best of things until one day you finally take notice, but by then it's too late. But the power of the Falls I believe, is what made their magic so terrible. It could not have done so much damage anywhere else.

"At first it was fairly innocent. Bringing a rainstorm on a shining summer day. Making a rabbit chase a dog, ferociously clacking it's teeth and wiggling its nose. But as they became aware of their power, the tricks became more mean-spirited. Little Davey grew a tail which, despite many surgeries, doctors were never able to get rid of. Jane, who always had buck teeth, grew long, sharp incisors and developed a fondness for using them to cut wood."

Josh had to rub his hands over his face to hide the laugh but Hansen was stone still.

"But the real damage came when they started hanging out at the old church when there weren't no services. That's when people started disappearing. Terrified whispers of black magic began. Once someone disappeared, they were never found again. Sometimes there would be pieces of clothing, a shoe, jewelry, things that would pop up in unexpected places long after a person went missing. There was never any hope to it, just an endless torment, an endless reminder of their absence and the terrible fear of what might have happened to them.

"Whispers and wailing filled the streets at night. People reported seeing ghosts. The fear was a tangible thing, a substance oozing around the city, bleeding from the walls. Churned out by the very Falls that used to offer protection. Many people had left by then and many more tried at that point. Some made it. For some, it was too late. The Falls had gone dark and just like a black hole sucking in everything within its gravitational pull, they swallowed everything, submerging it in the blackest night. The once perfect land became a prison. Those who remained, many of whom had stayed because they lost loved ones, became lost themselves.

"No one goes to Darkness Falls now. Not on purpose. Not to the town and 'specially not to the church. People who stumble their way in are lucky if they come out at all. The few that do, like old Jay- there's something not quite human about them. They've been tainted by the darkness."

The old guy paused a moment, looked around then headed to a dresser and yanked open a drawer. Pulled a flat bottle from it, took a swig, then another and screwed the cap back on replacing it, wiping his lips clean. He came back to the table, maybe trembling just a little and continued with his tale.

"Old Jay, he rambled on about time not following a linear path, not existing at all, life events jumbled up on top of each other in no particular order, moving forward and backward in time. He had no concept of his identity, no recollection of old Jay. Said he was two people, maybe more. Maybe he was for aught we know. He certainly picked up SOMETHING at Darkness Falls. His eyes would be open, staring at something nobody could see, living a different reality. In the shack where he was chained up they found hundreds of carvings in the walls; two letters, over and over. HJ. Over and over, then he disappeared. Probably back to Darkness Falls.

"It's a living thing, you know. Some monstrous evil. Helen and Dezi might've started it off, but I think it grew into something beyond their control. Something much worse. And it consumed them right along with everyone else. Us folks around here, we know it's still alive, even if it does slumber from time to time. And like any living thing, it's got to eat. Maybe not often. Like a snake, it swallows its food whole. Or a spider as it stores it up, making it last until it can lure in another victim. That's why we don't say much about Darkness Falls. Try to keep it secret or too boring to bother with. Maybe someday we'll be able to sort it out. Maybe."

O'Reilly fell silent, staring out into space. Josh was scrawling some notes as fast as he could. Hansen had stopped breathing, camera frozen in his hand. At last O'Reilly sighed and broke his reverie.

"We done good too, mostly. Every now and then we got someone foolish like you two, wants to go stir up what ought not be messed with. My advice," he said, nodding at the camera. "You've got your story. Best if you clear on out of here in the morning."

"Look," Hansen said the next morning, as the two men tumbled around the room, gathering their stuff. "Are you sure we still ought to go? I mean...given everything that we've learned?"

Josh looked at him in disbelief. Then he laughed. "Hansen, check your sources. We got that story from a drunken Irishman."

"So?" Hansen persisted.

"So..." Josh waved his hand around absently as he searched for his keys. "Don't they believe in leprechauns? Little folk? Even when they're not drunk?"

"Well...that doesn't make him wrong." Hansen shifted uncomfortably. "And Mary?"

Josh shrugged. "Seems like a sweet girl but, you know how it goes. If we want to get to the truth of the matter, we have to investigate this ourselves. That's what our whole show is about. If you want to cop out of this, we might as well sell our gig off to another team who has the guts to go where others won't."

Shaking his head after a long pause, Hansen grabbed his bag and headed to the car.

Darkness Falls was fifty miles out. At ten miles away, things started getting a little twitchy. Hansen couldn't decide if it was mist, haze or fog. Waterfalls, over-industrialization, witchcraft. Maybe all three, he decided. They drove in silence. He felt distinctly uneasy and glanced over at Josh, whose face was contorted with an emotion he was trying desperately to hide. Excitement. Of course he was excited.

Hansen sighed and turned his eyes forward. Was Josh right? Had he been too convinced by the fantastic tales at Outer Pass? As they drove forward, something began to emerge from the haze. Large gray rectangles.

"God," Josh exclaimed. "Those are without a doubt the ugliest buildings I've ever seen."

They undoubtedly were. Why anyone would plan to have those hideous, austere buildings as the welcoming committee to their town was beyond comprehension.

"Alright," said Hansen, grabbing his camera and stepping out of the car. Habit took over, the result of having done countless similar shoots. They had a job to do.

"Let me get some shots at the entrance of town. Maybe you can do a piece right there...'Welcome to Darkness Falls...'"

"Yeah, yeah, got it," Josh said, already striding away.

For the next few hours, they wandered through the town, taking footage of the vast apartment complexes, the steel mill that started the urbanization, grocery stores, abandoned apartments. Then up the hill to the old church, which was an eerie shade of black that Hansen couldn't believe was part of the original design.

As they stopped before the church to get their cover shot, Hansen noted a rushing in his ears. Puzzled, he cocked his head to one side, but couldn't determine a source. In fact, the more he thought of it, the more it dawned on him that he had been hearing the sound for a while now. Maybe since they entered the ancient town. It was like rushing water, like a river or...no, Hansen realized. It was a crashing. He was hearing a waterfall, maybe.

"Alright, only thing left to see is the Falls, or where the Falls used to be anyway," Josh said, turning his back on the church and heading to the car.

Hansen didn't follow. Something about the church raised the hairs on the back of his neck. He didn't want to be this close to that thing.

"Hey, Hansen. What are you doing?" Josh called.

Hansen blinked. He was standing on the little porch, just before the church's gaping door. Bewildered, he turned and stared down the stairs. Stairs he didn't remember climbing.

"Hansen!"

Hansen blinked in the dark interior of the church. Everything looked black and the shadows seemed to shift and slide, like the inky blackness was not just the absence of light, but an actual substance.

The air felt oily and thick. He went forward down the center aisle and Josh blindly followed nervously looking behind him. As if his hand didn't belong to him, it reached out, beneath the old and crumbling pulpit, and closed on the spine of a book. Slowly, he drew it out. The book seemed to glow with its own light. Not white, wholesome light, but a dim, sickly green light. Ancient, wicked looking symbols adorned the cover. Heart thudding, Hansen opened the book. Scribbled on the inside cover in a brownish-red ink were the names Helen Finn and Dezi Lars.

Hansen looked up and met Josh's horrified gaze. He seemed equally disturbed to find the book offering proof to the incredible story they had heard the night before and to find himself inside the church at all.

Old Jay, he rambled on about time not following a linear path, not existing at all, life events jumbled up on top of each other in no particular order, moving forward and backward in time.

Hansen shuddered. They both glanced down and saw Josh's hand fiercely gripping...a skull that was not in his hand a second ago. Josh made a choked sound as he dropped it. With the thud of the skull against the floorboards, the spell seemed to break and the air seemed to move. The entire church had seemed to carry a waiting quality. And they didn't want to wait anymore. In a rush, they both were out of the church, bounding down the stairs, running for all they were worth. Back through the village with its ugly buildings, but now they seemed more than a poor aesthetic choice. They seemed sinister.

It felt like something was chasing them. A cold wind on the back of their necks, a hot prickling fear. Hansen had never known such terror in his life. He sobbed in relief as he saw the car come into view. Beside him Josh was making a strangled, panting noise as they ran all out towards the car. For one heart stopping moment Hansen feared the doors would be locked, keys jangling, tauntingly out of reach. But the doors opened easily and the two men tumbled in. Josh jabbed his finger down on the lock button as Hansen screamed at him to "GO! GO! GO!"

Fumbling with the keys, Josh frantically found the ignition and turned the key, ready to speed out of there faster than he had ever driven in his life. Nothing happened. He jangled the keys, turning them back and forth repeatedly. With a slow, sick realization, he turned to face Hansen and saw his own horror mirrored back at him. They were stuck in Darkness Falls.

The sound of crashing water came closer and louder, thundering in on them as if they were under the waterfall itself. But there was no water, only the darkness. There was a sense of plummeting into the earth, as though the mud rose around them, the car sinking into something. And then a shadowy figure loomed before them. She pulled down her hood and the darkness was cut by the same sickly green light as the book had held, but this light was shining from her skull. The same skull that Josh had held in the church, animated by some terrible power. Josh gasped as the witch opened her jaws and an otherworldly shriek blasted from it. Josh and Hansen sat frozen as their eardrums shattered and their eyes went blank.

Their minds and bodies seemed to melt into each other, to become one with the darkness, with each other. Like a child pushing blobs of colored clay together. Compressing them, squishing them together. Melding together into one formed entity.

He had no concept of his identity, no recollection of old Jay. Said he was two people, maybe more. His eyes would be open, staring at something nobody could see, living a different reality. Carvings in the walls; two letters, over and over. HJ. Over and over...

HJ, HJ, HJ....

Hansen. Josh.

Darkness Falls had two new residents. Actually one.

THE ROYALTY OF HORROR

BOB MCNEIL

The muscular and tall sheriff, Butch Millstone, walked into the interrogation room wearing a tan uniform and Stetson hat. He stared contemptuously at the two men seated in front of a long metallic-silver desk, sipping his *frappe*. For no reason, other than a need to bully a weakling, he always hated a particular person in attendance.

Upon sitting, the sheriff yanked a folder from under his arm and slammed it down next to his plastic cup.

"Johnny Royal Pain in the Ass, I'm glad you could come down from your castle on the rock and talk to a lowly law enforcer."

"Butch, no one calls me that anymore," John Royal replied while finger-combing his dark brown mop-top haircut. He was nervous about looking at the sheriff's linebacker-broad body. Sweat surfed down John's back and his armpits. This fact was clear to anyone looking at his white Ramones T-shirt.

"Sorry, ever since our public-school days, the name stuck, much the same way that wasp stuck you in the butt during recess that one time."

"Damn it. I was eight. Let it go, will you?"

Athletic and strong even as a child, Butch always enjoyed bullying John. Almost every day, the big jock harangued and hit him.

"Mr. Royal, do not respond. Sheriff Millstone, this is harassment.

Either you confine yourself to the matters at hand, or we will leave. My client is under no obligation to be here now. Understand, we have better things to do on a Friday at six in the evening," Chuck Männer, the bald lawyer in the green suit said.

"Butch, enough, my attorney is right."

"Fine, so, John, you were informed about the three murders in the Citadel Stone community. New England never saw anything like them before. At each crime scene, a fan left paperback copies of your work. Unfortunately, the sicko knew enough to wear gloves. No DNA."

Angrily, Sheriff Millstone tossed a file. Large crime scene photos spilled out.

"Your novels are real novel. Some folks want to ban your books, I can see why. They bring out the best in folks."

"My client is fully aware of what transpired. And your sarcasm is unwarranted."

What a Hahvid masshole, Butch thought as he glared at the lawyer.

"Again, what do you want from him?" Chuck asked.

"We need Royal Pain's, I mean, Johnny's insights."

"Insights? What can I say? I'm just a writer."

Upon seeing the pictures, baked salmon, Jambalaya Rice, and asparagus wanted to catapult out of John's stomach. He stared at an image of a silver-haired pale-skinned man with a bashed-in head. About as gruesome, the next photographed crime scene revealed blood under some Slavic-looking guy's neck. Comparatively, the worst picture was that of a mangled brunette woman. The victim's face showed the fright in her frog-protruding eyes. John's dyspepsia worsened.

"The one murder is just like my novel *The Glimmering*, the killer clobbered a man to death. Did he use a polo stick?"

Butch nodded in agreement.

"Truth be told, I prefer the movie version. It's better than your book."

John and his lawyer looked at the sheriff with disdain. Satisfied that they made their point about Butch's insult, the writer continued speaking.

"Now, as for this other picture, judging from the wounds on this guy's neck, the killer siphoned his blood like in my novel *The Vampire's Acreage*. I am not sure about this photo, though."

"*Ayuh*, well, let me enlighten you. The perp put a pit bull in that old lady's *cah*."

"My God, *Cruel Joe*, my book about the crazed dog and the parked car."

"Don't forget about this last picture," Butch demanded.

Confused, John looked at a photo of a burnt house.

"Listen, I am sorry about the fire, but what does it have to do with my work?"

"A few feet away from the inferno, we found your first book."

"You're referring to *Connie*."

That novel, completed at the insistence of his wife, Gazelle, became John's first bestseller. The story about an abused teenage girl with the power of pyrokinesis held the number one position for a record sixty-six weeks.

"Here's a wicked *coinkydink*, these dead folks were all in the publishing business.

Do you recognize them?"

"No, I never met them."

Apprehensive that nervous incontinence would soil his blue jeans, John's legs shook.

"The old man who got his brains knocked in by the stick was H.P. Ambrose. Back around two decades ago, he published a speculative fiction magazine called *Extraordinary Stories Monthly*. That Eastern European guy, Sheridan Carmilla, was the fiction editor at one point for the same. Although it took a while, we identified the last poor victim as Shelley Byron. From all accounts, she served as a copy editor. They were just old retired nerds that exercised their jaws at libraries, *Dunkies*, or a friend's *pahlah*. Sometimes they'd walk from H.P.'s house, the first victim, by the way, that's the place that looks like an ashtray now, and make a *packie* run together."

"My God," John muttered to himself as he held his hands over his face.

Suddenly, without an announcement, the writer stood up. Unable to endure everything said, he ran out of the room.

"Where are ya goin'? This here interrogation is not over yet," Butch yelled.

"Can't you see that this whole thing upset my client?" Chuck said.

"Oh, dear, tell your sensitive client to stay in town. We may have some follow-up questions for him. Who knows, maybe the killer will use Johnny's recent book for inspiration. Then, again, perhaps not. That last title, *The Bobby Rockers*, was a stinker. Accordin' to what I heard, that pharmacy and booze head got tanked when he wrote it," the sheriff bellowed for John and all those outside the interrogation room to hear.

They came out of the room. Dumbstruck by the noise, deputies, civilians, and a secretary looked at the lawyer and the sheriff."

"There is no evidence connecting him to these crimes. Therefore, until you produce a warrant, John can go where he damn well pleases. Goodnight, sheriff."

"Question: Do you know why flies love every lawyer's mouth? Answer: It's because they enjoy the crap that you guys spew."

Infuriated, the lawyer searched for his client. He was standing head down in the lobby of the station.

"John, wait up, let's talk outside."

Ignoring the lawyer, John rushed towards the exit. Deputies, while seated at desks, gawked at the thin 6'4 writer. John's wife looked stunned by the commotion. Sitting on a steel bench outside, the chubby ponytail-wearing brunette in the gray jumpsuit waited for her husband's explanations.

"John, you look pallid. Sit down and tell me what's wrong."

"God, I got to get out of here."

"Fine, sweetheart, let's go home."

Rapidly, the lawyer, John, and his wife walked towards their car. From the top of the landing, the sheriff yelled. The sound of his explosive voice made John and his associates turn around.

"Hey, Shakespeare, I'll be here workin' on the murderous facts that your fiction created."

Disgusted and surprised by Butch's words, the trio stormed off.

"That hick understands the law as well as I understand rocket science. Disregard him. He won't harass you anymore," his lawyer assured him.

"Thanks for being here with us, but right now, I just want to go home with my wife."

"I understand, no problem. If you need me, call."

On that October night, pedestrians stared at John Royal the same way they would a rock star. Many of whom wanted an autograph. Concerned about losing their literary idol, the fans made a circle around the lawyer and the Royals. Fanatically, they waited for a chance to speak to John.

Somewhere within the growing crowd, there was a dirty, unshaven bum who did not look like a fan. That man, wearing a Red Sox baseball cap, stained gray t-shirt, and tattered blue jeans, had a hateful countenance. By his left leg, being held with a leash, a dark brown Pitbull stood and stared. Besides those observations, John swore that he recognized him.

The reason why John did not fear the growing crowd was because of Gunner, his driver, who also served as a bodyguard. Fortunately, the tall, Nordic, retired kickboxer waited by the Royal's Genesis G90 a few feet away. Only a masochist would have challenged the athletic thirty-year-old.

Annoyed by the masses, Chuck shoved his way through the autograph adulators. Young, as well as old females and males of different races, all got a push from the bodyguard's shoulders.

Even though Gazelle became an award-winning author, her presence there was equivalent to the opening act for the Beatles. Long ago, she accepted her husband's fame and the way it eclipsed her critically acclaimed efforts.

"Mr. Royal," a chubby, pimple-faced girl said, "I love your books. May I have your autograph?"

Upset about the sheriff's report and overwhelmed by the worshippers, John walked away.

"Please forgive me, but this is not a good time."

John and his wife were ushered into the backseat of their luxurious automobile. Outside the windows, the passengers and driver heard these statements of disapproval:

"What an egotistical prick."

"I didn't like his last book anyway."

"He's so full of himself his stomach must suffer from indigestion."

"*Fuhggedabout* it, his work is so formulaic."

"Yeah, and a lot of his stories are politically incorrect."

Traveling away from the station and the town did not affect John's need for communication. Patiently, his wife waited for a private moment so they could talk about all that happened.

Twenty minutes later as they pulled up to the entrance of the remote-controlled driveway gate, John said, "Gunner, take the rest of the evening off. We'll walk from here."

Monosyllabic as ever, the driver said yes, let his employers out, and put the car in the garage.

Confident that a walk up to their red Edwardian mansion would rouse a conversation, Gazelle awaited her husband's usual wittiness. Amusingly, when they first purchased the home, John referred to it as the ginger cracker with wifely sweetness.

This time no joke came from him.

"John, what's going on?"

"Give me a sec. I am trying to figure a way to tell you something, that's all."

Avoiding his two prepubescent sons and daughter, John took long strides over to his office. Zombie-eyed with anxiousness, the writer closed his door after telling his kids not to disturb him. The children that favored both parents, felt slighted by their father's dismissiveness.

More tactfully, Gazelle crouched and spoke to their children.

"Daddy doesn't feel well. Go outside and play. I'll join you later."

Free of their presence, Gazelle entered the Regency-Era-styled office.

"John, relax and tell me what the hell is going on."

"You know about the murders."

"Doesn't everybody?"

"About those publishers, I knew them, well, sort of in a limited way."

"What?"

"Listen, my father, before abandoning my mother, older brother, and me, he used to write pulp fiction. He submitted his work to a particular publication he loved over and over again. Each time, without variation, he received rejection letters for his effort from *Extraordinary Stories Monthly*. Those murdered people all worked for that now-defunct magazine."

"My God, that's terrible. Where are you going with this? I mean, it's a weird coincidence, right?"

"Honey, sit down, please. You love me, right?"

"Of course, I do. Why ask me that now?"

"What if I told you I kind of plagiarized my first four books?"

"Stop! You're joking."

"I wish I were. Around the time of my brother's eleventh birthday, when I was six, my dad went out for some beer and never came back. Besides leaving us brokenhearted, he left tons of unfinished manuscripts. The stories weren't the worst. They just needed a lot of edits. My father, although a very creative person, didn't do so well in writing classes. Ma said he didn't even finish the first semester of college. He preferred to spend his days drinking booze and pounding out his stories on a Smith Corona typewriter. Nonetheless, my mom, who worked as a maid, loved that always-unemployed ne'er do well. His donnybrooks and frequent arrests for drunken disorderly behavior did not diminish her loyalty to him."

"Wait, are you telling me your father, Edward, wrote those books? How could you?"

"Well, I improved them when I reached adulthood. By that, I mean, because of my editing, the stories were publishable."

"Oh God, I am so disappointed in you." Gazelle rubbed her temples with both hands. "My head hurts. I feel sick. Did you do it for fame and fortune? We didn't need those things. I was happy when you were just a High School English teacher. We lacked money, but I still loved you. What about all those poems dedicated to me? Did you write them?"

"Honestly, sweetheart, believe me, I actually wrote those."

"Your poems, especially the ones about your brother's passing and mom's deaths due to cancer, touched me. You could've created your own stories as well."

"Retooling my father's stories made me feel like he was still a part of my life. In a way, we became collaborators."

"So, let me get this straight, by age 26, you were re-edited his work."

"No, actually, I was 25. The first book wound up getting published a year later. Once it became a bestseller, I couldn't stop myself from working on more of them."

"I've been married to you since we were nineteen. And in those fifteen years, you never told me any of this. Damn it, John, you're a stranger to me. Man, I need a drink."

Forlorn, John walked to his bookcase with a voluminous collection of works. Behind the first edition of the *Lost Weekend*, he retrieved a bottle of whiskey.

"I thought your drinking days were behind you."

"Sorry, I'll throw it away."

"Like hell, you will. Give me the bottle. Forget about a glass. It will slow me down."

Two swigs later, Gazelle asked, "What in God's name does your plagiarism have to do with the murders?"

"That I don't know. But what I can say is, my father submitted excerpted versions of those books to *Extraordinary Stories Monthly*. The killer must have read them and imitated the plots."

Startled by the ringing phone, the couple jumped.

"Don't answer that damn thing, please," John pleaded.

"It may be the sheriff." Fatigue made Gazelle put the call on speakerphone. "Hello, with whom am I speaking?"

"Get John. Put him on the horn," a gravelly voice demanded.

"Tell me who you are, and I may," Mrs. Royal replied.

"Fine, tell him this:

From childhood's hour I have not been
As others were—I have not seen
As others saw—I could not bring

My passions from a common spring—
From the same source I have not taken
My sorrow—I could not awaken
My heart to joy at the same tone—
And all I lov'd—I lov'd alone. . ."

Convinced the call was a prank, Gazelle was about to hang up. John leaped and stopped her.

"Who the, who the--?" John screamed.

"Oh, so you're there. Do you remember I used to recite that poem all the time? Mostly, I did it after belting back a bottle of whiskey."

"Dad? Is that you?"

"Meet me at the Schlomo mansion. Be there in an hour. Come alone, no wife, no police, do you understand?"

"Ahh- Yes, sir."

Not even sixty seconds passed from the time he hung up the phone to when he made his way to the door.

"Just because of a poem, you're going to meet this guy."

"Don't get me wrong Gazelle, I am worried. Nonetheless, your concern, although justified, won't stop me."

"How the hell do you even know it's your father?"

"Never in an interview, story, or essay did I ever mention my father's favorite poet. Dad, many years ago, was obsessed with Poe."

"Do you know what's even disturbing? Why is he getting in contact with you now? To be safe, we should call the sheriff."

"No, don't call him or anybody for that matter," John demanded, "You heard what he said."

"Just tell me where you're going."

"I'll tell you if you promise not to inform anybody about it."

"Fine, I won't mention a thing."

"Remember when we were dating, I took you once to an old abandoned house where stoners sometimes hung out and sold pot."

Allowed a moment to think, both John and Gazelle remembered the huge German Gothic slate-colored building in the nasty town of Darkness Falls. It was once owned by the venerated Austrian neurologist and psychoanalyst Dr. Frederick Schlomo overlooking the now dried up river, the house, and the three acres surrounding it were the subject of many urban legends.

The doctor, his wife, and six daughters lived in that oversized opulent abode for years. Around 1909, the famed doctor died suddenly in his home. The wife sold off some of the land to survive but debt, coupled with depression, soon killed his family off one by one and followed him grave-ward. Time demolished the surrounding neighborhood. City officials, against the desires of real estate developers, fought to declare the house a landmark with the hope of it becoming a museum. Rampat bureaucracy left the place vacant for decades and the manor became a nest for animals and a refuge for stoners, homeless and horny people without the funds for a hotel.

"Back in our rebellious years, I brought you there and we had the one wonderful experience in that old house, didn't we?" John sadly reminisced.

"Yes, I remember. You brought me there to scare me into sleeping with you."

"And it worked."

Perhaps for all of a second, the couple forgot the murderer using John's books as inspiration and the unexpected phone call from the man claiming to be his father. Thought back to a time when they were truly happy.

"I don't know why I did that to this day. I swore there was a ghost there. I heard things that you didn't. Don't go there! Please. You know what they say about Darkness Falls. People who go there don't come back."

That overshadowed the memory with realization. John looked at her gravely, "I have to."

"That isn't the place to meet a man who you haven't seen since your youth. Don't do this. Tell him to meet you in a more public location, in another town."

Disregarding requests to stay, John walked towards the front door. "Please, I beg you. Don't tell anybody about what's going on. Under no circumstances tell that buffoon with a badge, Butch, about the phone call. I will handle this matter myself. Can you promise?"

"God, John, please be careful."

Gazelle's uttered words felt like the medicine she spat in a napkin behind her mother's back. Physical and mental pain overwhelmed the stressed wife. She feared for her husband.

John drove his own car. A 1958 green Plymouth Fury he lavishly purchased with the earnings of his second best seller. Had his day gone differently, John would have stopped and mused about nature. But he was unmoved by the autumn scenery of yellowish leaves and emerald-green lawns, he only thought about the parent who abandoned him as a child. Where there was a park or stream, a memory of Edward Royal stood. Often compared to rockabilly greasers, the tall and broad brown-haired patriarch, between alcohol binges and hours of typing, sometimes played ball with his sons in those very same parks.

Then he entered Darkness Falls.

John veered off the main road, took side streets he remembered from his past, deeper into the town that locals said had been haunted for a hundred years. He'd heard all those rumors as a teenager but never put any stock in them. Yet as he drove further into Darkness Falls a shadow seemed to loom over him that he never felt before. He still had more concerns about leaving his vintage car parked in the vacant lot in front of the mansion than any spirits that might be present. The ominous structure did not assuage his apprehension about what he was about to do. If a single building had ever repre-sented a place better than this, he couldn't imagine it.

Alone in the night, fear became his navigator as he walked along the unkempt grounds of the estate. Each step concealed a threat. Holes, logs, and rocks did not announce their whereabouts. Feral animals gazed from the brush at the stumbling writer and wondered why he ventured into their domain. Those eyes. Some of them did not look like they were from any forest creature.

Unsureness slowed his pace as he approached the entrance of the house.

Not in need of an invitation or keys, John pushed tall medieval-style twin doors. Manic barking from somewhere inside greeted his arrival. The dread of sharp teeth made him reconsider going any farther.

Even in the darkness, he saw a wooden double staircase. Steps worthy of aristocratic shoes went up to four floors. Resulting from exploration years ago, the writer remembered the numerous rooms. Houseguests, years ago, specifically famous doctors, and philosophers knew the amenities of the accommodations as well. Unwilling to walk up, he stared at the tinkling chandelier that swung unsteadily as a result of a draft. Filth tarnished stained glass windows composed of mosaic angels and forked- tongued demons. Surprisingly neither impact cracks nor dirt could diminish the windows' majestic-ness. The same did not apply to the walls. Graffiti-blemished surfaces left John wondering why bored kids invested creative time marring walls with indecipherable words. He looked higher up and found the hole-riddled roof revealed thunderstorm clouds.

From the living room, a liquor-and-tobacco-wrecked voice demanded, "Come in, kid. Don't fear ole Chomper. He's chained to a pillar in the basement. Shut up, dog. You'll meet our dinner guest later."

Obediently the animal stopped its need for noise.

Awestruck, John saw the canine's master. He appeared to have a bare pate with gray, wiry hair on the sides. Something about his face was familiar but from his very recent past.

It's the guy from the crowd outside the police station, John remembered.

"Stop ogling like a writer and follow me, Gut Glutman."

Those words removed doubts about identity. John, during a chubby period, got dubbed with that nickname by his father.

"Dad, it's you."

"Come in and see the guy who sired you," Edward Royal said.

By the light of a kerosene lamp on the ground in the parlor, John saw his father clearly.

"Yeah, kid, I didn't age like some pampered celebrity. Having a fortune kept you fit. Poverty is a screwworm. It ate the life out of me."

Seemingly embarrassed over his baldness, the old man retrieved his baseball cap from his back pocket and jammed it on. He was gaunt and worn down like an old stone statue.

"Ah, Dad, I would've helped you out financially."

"Oh, of course, you would've of, off the money made from my ideas."

"I am sorry about that. I thought you'd be proud–"

"Damn you and your apology. You took my old rejected stories and re-edited them. Maybe my poor education didn't understand passive sentences, dangling modifiers, and that other schoolboy crap. Nevertheless, my ideas had something beyond pedantic lessons. They had excitement. They were great stories!"

"I apologized for using your work. But you left it, like you left me. Can you apologize for abandoning your family?"

"Looking at you and your mother after each failure hurt worse than a kick in a nutsack. I failed in college, my jobs, my marriage, and my ability to be a father. Honestly, what smashed my manhood the most was bombing as a writer. Creative writing was going to be my rocket off this toilet of a planet."

"Leaving our family was cruel."

"It wasn't too cruel after all because I left those manuscripts of mine. If not for me, you wouldn't have a writing career. I don't feel guilty about abandoning a domestic life that was strangling me. Nor do I feel guilty about killing all those philistines at that magazine."

"What?"

"I would've fried those eggheads sooner. Unfortunately, a stretch for attempted manslaughter at the Shapak Prison stopped my plan. My first foray didn't go so well. But the new digs did provide a great view of your castle. Seeing it from barred windows inspired my escape."

"This is another one of your stories, right."

"The only thing made-up here is your literary career. Well, this is the denouement."

By the end of that statement, his father pulled out a Beretta Bobcat from his pocket and aimed it at John's head.

"Don't kill me. I'm your son."

"I could've molded a greater descendant out of a ream of paper."

"I'll split my profits with you. That will get you set up, back on your feet."

"To hell with that! And to hell with you."

The sight of the raised gun could not make John move. Fear epoxied him to the floor.

Behind the scared writer, creaking sounds indicated that someone was approaching. The appearance of another intruder inspired the dog's barking rage.

"Who's over there? Did you bring somebody, you yellow-backed hack?"

All of a sudden, Edward saw the owner of the heavy-footed gait. Panic bleached the color out of the old man's face.

"Drop your friggin' gun now," Butch's welcomed yell demanded.

"Screw you, hayseed."

Succumbing to his need for survival, John ducked behind a dusty sheet covered chair.

Torn between shooting John as he bolted or at the Sheriff, Edward hesitated. That second-long indecision was just what the law enforcer needed. A succession of bullets from Butch's Sig Sauer P226 riddled the old man and he collapsed into darkness. He stepped over to check that he was down and would stay down. Killing a psychopath in a former psychoanalyst's house was the definition of irony for the Sheriff. Furthermore, seeing various wounds in the serial killer's heart gave Butch the gratification that any drug or drink could not. While the corpse laid on the floor, he had the notion of shooting him a few more times. But concern about John's reaction prevented the usage of more bullets.

Various questions about a single thing pierced John's mind as he peered from his hiding place. Did Gazelle betray her promise, or did Butch follow him? Either way could he be mad? And was his dad's death more grievous because of who caused it? Wasn't this close to a scene out of his last book?

Reluctantly despite being concerned with the growling dog's location, the sheriff put his gun back in its holster.

"My old man wasn't worth the salt on my brow either. Some reunions should never happen as we both now know," Butch confessed, thinking he might have excised some of his own demons as well. He walked over to where John unsteadily stood.

Right there and then, for the first time, Butch did not think of John as a bookish nebbish who deserved years of harassment but as a kindred spirit who had overcome bad parental entanglement. It was clear he needed somebody to lean on right at that moment.

Except for the brief lamentation over losing his father twice, John felt comfort in the long arms that caught him as he fainted into the dark.

THE QUIET ONES

LIAM SPINAGE

"Five more last night." Arlette's voice was tired, scratchy. Jacques looked up from his patient in concern, not just for Arlette's voice but for the voices of so many others.

"That brings us to twenty-two." Jacques' broad shoulders slumped momentarily. He'd been up for thirty hours straight now. He knew he had to get some rest. He also knew that rest wouldn't come. Not until he had an answer.

"How can twenty-two people suddenly lose their voice?" Arlette's query was spattered with a light raspy cough and muted by the handkerchief she held over her mouth as she spoke. "What do you think, doctor?"

"I don't know. It's possible there's a natural explanation. I'm not entirely convinced until I do some more tests."

Arlette narrowed her brow and turned her head away slightly. She'd been working with Jacques at the Hope Springs Mission for a couple of months now and thought she had the feel of the man. He rarely spoke and even when he did, there was much he didn't say. She'd come to understand that what he didn't say was just as important as what he did. If he wasn't convinced there was a natural explanation for a sudden outbreak of what might well be laryngitis, then that meant he thought something else was at work. Namely, a super-natural element. That made it her territory, not his.

"I'll ask around. See what people know. At least, the part that they're willing to say."

Jacques nodded wearily. At this rate there wouldn't be anyone left who could say anything, willingly or otherwise. There were few enough people in Darkness Falls as it was. Most of those were troubled and traumatized. Perhaps that's what had drawn him here in the first place. From a young age, he had wanted to be a doctor. No, scratch that, what he had really wanted to be was a healer. There was a subtle difference in those words. He wanted to make people better, make the world a better place. It seemed fitting that he'd been assigned here, that the world had responded by putting him in a place where people really needed him. He stifled a yawn and walked over to the sink to wash his hands.

Arlette stepped outside the mission and looked down the street. At one end was the edge of town, where the road petered out into abandoned fields full of rotting corn stretched across the valley floor. She had thought about treading that road many times. Of getting out, like so many did. Somehow, she never managed to take that first step. There always seemed to be something drawing her back in. Behind the mission was the remains of what she once understood to be the lake, the crater caked now in a red-brown sludge of mud and rust. Even the spring which had given the mission its name had dried up. It was as if even fresh water - hell, anything fresh, wanted nothing to do with the eternal seeping entropy and decay which inculcated itself into every sinew, every fiber of one's being if one had been here long enough.

Arlette had been here three years.

In the other direction lay the mass of squalid shanties which sepa-rated them from what she liked to call the heart of darkness - the largely abandoned town center where the buildings were tall enough to cast long shadows over the rest of the town and where people rarely ventured these days. Everything salvageable or stealable had already been taken years ago. There was little left to loot. Arlette set off toward those shanties, past the boarded-up gas station and across alleys strewn with broken glass and equally broken lives. She knew who she'd approach first to try and get an answer. She only hoped she'd get there in time.

When he'd first rolled up here, the name of the mission caused Jacques to break out in a rare wry smile. There were no springs here anymore where the mountain had once given up its waters in torrents to feed the lake below. He knew enough geology to understand where those falls must once have been, how majestic they must once have looked. Once he'd gone inside the dilapidated building and found it empty, he also understood there wasn't much hope either.

What there was, still, was a mission. Not capitalized as it was on the creaking sign which hung half-heartedly outside the place, but the mission he'd felt a calling to all his life. He'd tried to leave his own demons behind when he'd left Canada, but they had followed him incessantly, hounding his every move. Very well, he decided. Time to pick a battleground and meet them head on. Within days, he'd managed to salvage a few essential medical supplies. One day later, he had his first patient. Three days later, that patient had become a conspirator against the darkness in his own life, just as he had in hers. When Arlette had first walked into the mission, her arms had been crisscrossed with bloody scratches so much that he'd feared a serious infection. Even then, she'd refused to say what had caused them. She hadn't needed to. As their eyes met in a flash of under-standing, he knew they were somehow self-inflicted. He'd eventually teased an answer out of her, but that answer had come with addi-tional questions. Fearful dreams, dark thoughts. Long screams in the night borne of a pain she carried inside which she felt compelled to make manifest on her body as she struggled against what she'd found here.

"Here be monsters." She had pointed toward the town as they sat outside the mission. "And here," she admitted, pointing to her head.

"And here," pointing to his. Jacques merely nodded and they'd watch the sun go down and darkness fall, hand in hand, then arm in arm.

A lot had happened since then. Jacques didn't really understand what Arlette meant about the darkness in the heart of town. He'd assumed she was talking metaphorically. Now, he was sure she wasn't.

He had two patients with severe burns and no more painkillers. And twenty-two patients with what looked like laryngitis but wasn't. There was no cough, no splutter. What he could see when they tried to speak wasn't the exhaustion of someone with an illness, it was the exasperation of someone who can't express anything but fear, confusion and anger.

Jacques had had some success with calming them down, getting them to write what they needed on paper. There were a few problems here though. It seemed that Darkness Falls hadn't attracted a literate crowd. Hardly surprising. Many of his patients struggled to read and write at the best of times, but when they were in this state, they found it even more difficult to articulate. To top it all, the paper got moldy quickly. Ink dried up at an alarming rate. Pencil leads broke almost every time they were used. It was frustrating.

Currently, he was encountering that frustration first-hand in the person of Davey Winters who didn't need a larynx or a pen to tell Jacques just what he thought of him. Not when he had two huge fists to do the talking for him.

Arlette, meanwhile, had stopped to catch her breath at a dime store a few blocks over. Here, Sara was busy setting out the stalls outside and swatting off the bluebottles that had begun to buzz around angrily. She did this every morning with a blend of defiance and precision which Arlette found comforting. Sara was the only person Arlette knew who'd been here longer than her, which as far as she knew made her the longest-standing resident of Darkness Falls. Sometimes, Arlette wondered what kept her here. Deep down though, she knew the answer. Like so many others, Sara simply had nowhere else to go.

She looked over at the display of goods Sara had available. The usual array of scavenged parts, the few unlabeled tins of presumably-food. Arlette had bought one of those tins once and it had turned out to be rice pudding. She wasn't a fan, but had eaten it anyway, straight from the tin with a little spoon she kept in a makeshift pocket which was little more than a tear in the lining of her fleece.

"Hi Sara. How's things?"

Sara smiled and waved Arlette closer. She was normally more talkative than this. Unless…

Damn it all. You were my last chance.

Sara pointed at her throat and shrugged as Arlette swore quietly under her breath.

"You wanna come down to the mission and let Jacques have a look at it?"

Sara shook her head, her dreadlocks whipping animatedly as she did.

"Ain't no point," she seemed to say. After a protracted series of points and gestures, Arlette understood. "We both know that what's doing this ain't something he can fix."

"You got any ideas?" Sara saw and heard a lot as she scavenged her way through the city. Things that might be crucial to understanding how to deal with this. Or at least understand where it was coming from.

Sara shook her head again, then appeared to change her mind. She beckoned Arlette inside the shop. Arlette followed, knowing that if nothing else there would be good coffee.

Jacques managed to dodge the first blow but succumbed to the next two. Say what you like about Davey, but he still had a good right hook. Both their faces were contorted now, Davey's with rage and Jacques' with pain. Fumbling in a pocket, Jacques staggered backwards and managed to steady himself momentarily on the edge of a nearby cot before the flurry of Davey's blows became almost too much to bear. One punch sent him reeling across the floor, arms raised over his face in defense, giving him a few precious moments to extract the syringe from his pocket. Now all he had to do was get in close enough to use it without causing any further harm to either of them. As Davey loomed over him, red-faced and panting, Jacques thought he saw his chance and reached up, grabbing hold of the thin cotton of Davey's blood-stained shirt and dragging him down on top of him. When he went to administer the sedative, though, Davey countered with a jarring head-butt which knocked it out of his hand. The pair of them rolled around on the floor for what seemed like an age, neither of them landing any blows, just trying to disentangle themselves from each other. Davey grabbed him in a choke hold, threatening to draw out the last of Jacques' breath just as his own had been cruelly stolen from him. He was about to pass out when he felt Davey suddenly go limp on top of him, drool forming at the corner of his mouth. As he rolled the uncon-scious Davey off him, there stood a smiling Arlette, syringe in hand. His savior.

"Sara's lost her voice too."

They'd managed to pick up Davey between them and deposit his body unceremoniously on a makeshift bed. He'd recover soon enough, but they'd have some time to deal with the root cause. Jacques just hoped that time would be enough.

"I can't imagine Sara ever being quiet." Jacques winced as Arlette applied a cloth to his head wound.

"I know what you mean. Still, she showed me something on the map. She's seen something over at the old civic center. Here, look, she gave us an artist's impression." Arlette unfolded a sheet of paper and showed it to Jacques. It looked like the after-impression of a Rorschach test, all blotchy interlocking circles in shades of gray. Jacques wasn't sure whether to be impressed at the artist's hand he didn't know Sara had or to recoil in abject horror that this arrangement of muted, faded shapes might be something which had a physical presence in the town he'd come to call home.

Arlette watched him chew this over in his mind as she passed him a dented styrofoam cup of coffee she'd brought back from the shop for her.

"Here, soldier, reckon you'll need this."

"Thanks." Jacques downed it on one, desperate to be more alert if not more refreshed. He winced.

"It's not that bad!" Arlette's gentle jibe woke him more than the coffee had.

"It's awful!"

"I guess you just get used to it. It's the best we got."

They both paused.

"You're going over, aren't you?"

Another pause, longer this time.

"We. We're going over. I'm not doing this alone; I'll need you there with me. Whatever it is, we'll deal with it. Besides, do you want to be here when Davey comes round?"

Jacques groaned.

"Thought not. We'd best get a move on if we're going to get there and back before dark."

It seemed he had little choice in the matter.

"Why do you do it?"

They'd reached the three-story civic hall and paused while they looked for the best way inside. The main doors stood impressively intact in their off-white marble with Greek columns on either side, laced with little cracks that had taken their toll over the years but still standing tall. Above them, a clock hung over the main entrance. It had long been abandoned by its hands and numbers. Just another faceless entity in the town, a reminder of what grandeur had lived here once.

"Why do I do what?" Jacques knew what Arlette meant. They'd had this conversation before, many times.

"Help people." Arlette spat in the road, her phlegm thick with the strong, black, awful coffee.

"You know why. They need it."

"OK, so why don't you help yourself while you're at it? Physician, heal thyself, right?"

"I can't. At least, not like that.

Arlette decided to change tack.

"Need to heal everyone else first, right? Like you're the Fisher King?"

"Well, this is certainly the Wasteland." Jacques managed a laugh, then retorted. "Why do you do it?"

"Why do I do what?" Arlette was enjoying the circular conversation.

"Keep looking. Investigating. What do you hope to find?"

"What makes you so sure there's something there to find? Ready to believe in the supernatural finally, man of science?"

"Spare me your jabs of mockery!" Jacques laughed again, but his face became serious. "I'm ready, I think. This place…" He didn't need to say any more. As if in response, what sun managed to permeate the low hanging mist had firmly retreated behind a looming array of murky gray clouds.

"Right on cue." That's what Arlette intended to say, but it came out differently. What she actually said was "……"

Jacques looked up, wide awake now. "Arlette?"

Arlette was frantically trying to indicate something to him, but he wasn't sure what. He thought - out of the corner of his eye - that he saw the tiniest shadow escape from the corner of her mouth and zigzag its way to the marble doors, only to get lost in the rest of the shadows. Surely a trick of the light? No, he said to himself. He had to be ready to believe.

First, though, he had another patient to deal with.

Arlette had collapsed to the ground in one of her frequent coughing fits but managed to recover quickly enough and shot him a scathing look which he interpreted as "Are you ready now?" She then produced two flashlights from her fleece and handed one to him. He rolled it over in his hand and tested it by twisting the end. It flickered briefly but shone well enough. Arlette had done the same.

They both nodded to each other and climbed the stairs to the marble doors. They didn't need words to understand each other's intentions. Not anymore.

It took their combined strength to lever the door open even a fraction, but that was enough to let them in. They looked around, flashlights gleaming paths. In the mist-choke darkness, these little paths of light showed long-forgotten pews, signs and documents. Whatever order might once have held sway here, it had long departed and left in its wake a ramble of rubble, all discarded bureaucracy of former lives. Human beings were not meant to enter these doors, not anymore. No sun or moon entered here. Nothing did any more. The central hall was silent as the grave but so much worse. The grave, after all, holds either the promise of finality or the chance of another life, a better life, an afterlife. There was no such hope here.

Arlette threw a pebble at Jacques to attract his attention. He was shivering in the sudden cold, standing there open-mouthed.

Snap out of it!

Jacques tried to speak. Tried to articulate what it was he was looking at. To put it into words. All that came to mind was all the voices from his past which had wounded him. His abusive father. Angry patients. An angrier girlfriend. They all told him the same. He was never going to amount to anything. He was useless. He was wrong. He was a waste of space.

All the voices said that, except one. Somewhere, somehow, amidst the sound and fury, one voice rang clear. It was Arlette's.

"Believe!"

And he did. Not just in the amorphous, slowly circling shapes which seemed to be edging forward towards him. Not just in the supernatural and otherworldly explanations which his rational mind had always wanted to dismiss.

For the first time in ages. Jacques believed in himself.

It was an absolute rush. He screamed out loud, all the repressed fury and rage and guilt within him came out in one long breath as he reached up to wipe the tears away from his eyes.

The form stopped moving.

He screamed again - louder than before - and Arlette's voice joined him, suddenly found, camaraderie in cacophony. Hundreds of voices then flitted between them, every soul silenced now released in a bitter, primal scream with only one message to convey. "No more," it said. Not as a plea, but as a rallying cry. "No more."

The monstrous form shifted in the shadows, turned, and gave flight. Jacques fell to the floor exhausted, and Arlene collapsed again alongside him, gasping with newly found breath. It would appear that for the time being that they had won out.

The darkness would come again, as it always did. But neither Jacques nor Arlette were willing to go gentle into that good night. Not while there was still hope.

All Hail the New Killer

BRIAN STIEGLITZ

Clive bought his first can of pepper spray a few weeks after he and Oscar started talking again. He didn't think he'd ever need to use it, but his mind would conjure up scenarios where he did. Sometimes it even went back to the moment that made him buy one – the night when he didn't realize that the man who approached him in the bathroom had been following him back to his train. If he'd had one it would have been a quick pull from his pocket, turn of the cap, then a gentle push, and before he could say "Get your hands off—"

"AAAARRRGGGHHHH WHAT THE HELL YOU BASTAAAR-RGGGHHH!"

That was as far as Clive's imagination went.

He'd probably shake uncontrollably or maybe even break down crying if he did that. Part of him would have to fight the urge to say sorry and call for help, or ask someone for water or, or – no, wait. It's milk isn't it? Yeah, he remembered reading that in some social media post a few years back.

"Milk huh? I guess that makes sense since you drink it after eating peppers anyway," Oscar's voice said from the phone Clive rested in the cupholder of his sedan. The speaker phone and echo from the plastic cylinder made his voice sound weird, not like he remembered.

But Clive didn't use pepper spray that night. He stood peering over his shoulder and hoping the man would stop following him. Then an MTA employee stepped in between them. He didn't want to think about what might have happened if they were alone.

"Do you think anybody's ever tried, like, putting pepper spray on their food?" Clive shouted at the cup holder with a chuckle.

"Dude, honestly, I wouldn't be surprised if that became the next Tide Pod challenge. Seriously don't do it though, you might die—"

"I wasn't going to! I'm not that dumb," Clive said.

"Okay good, just checking. But … uh … it's a good thing you have it. And you would have been right to use it at the train station if that guy had put a finger on you—"

"I know, I—"

"You can't wait for someone else to step in and intervene … even if there's someone there. You have to defend yourself the second you get the chance or it will be too late."

"Thanks for the pep talk Oz. I mean, you're right, but I can't stand the thought of hurting someone," Clive said with conviction.

Throughout his whole life, he always wanted, needed, people to approve of him – his family, his friends, even strangers. That's why he never got into a fist fight with anyone at school. He got hit or pushed a few times. But whenever one of the jocks or bullies would pick on him, he'd stay quiet. He stayed quiet a lot. Other times, he'd just run as fast as he could.

That's what happened when he and Oscar tried dating the first time. They had seen each other for about three months when they were juniors in college. Clive would sneak into Oscar's bedroom like they were teenagers in a 90s rom com. He could still see the Green Day poster on the back of Oscar's bedroom door. He could picture the half empty cologne bottles and polaroid photos on his dresser that sat next to a weathered glass bowl and a toilet paper roll affixed with a dryer sheet that they used to breath weed into to hide the smell.

Clive was leaving the bathroom one night when Oscar's older brother came charging into their house like a drunken hurricane. They locked glazed eyes for a split second before the towering behemoth stormed into his brother's room. Clive charged out of the house as fast as he could, slurred screams echoing behind him, because he knew about Oscar's brother's narrow-mindedness.

"I don't think anyone likes hurting people . . . except for, like, sociopaths and serial killers." The way Oscar said that was really not like him. Kind of spooky. "But sometimes you need to do it, if you have to protect yourself – or someone else," he said.

Clive paused for a second, hoping Oscar wasn't thinking of the same memory as him. Then he almost habitually felt the pepper spray in his jacket pocket, right next to his inhaler and EpiPen. It made his heart race to touch. In a way, it was exposure therapy.

"Yeah, I guess you're right."

The morning after he ran out of Oscar's house, Clive tried texting him – to no avail. Then he called. Nothing. He tried the next day too, and the next. Then he saw Oscar pass him on campus with a black eye. That was the last time they saw each other for two years.

Years later, Clive saw a familiar face appear on a dating app. Fast forward two months and he was driving to meet his former flame for the first time since college – but in a new city. No homophobic brothers, no bigoted parents. It was the fresh start he so desperately wanted for them.

Clive turned off a highway and onto a skinny street as the setting sun spilled through a few gutted buildings that looked like they hadn't been used in years. Daylight seemed like it was dimming faster than usual as the sunset cast ominous shadows against rows of duplexes along side streets that led into the heart of the city.

"Sooooo ... how do you like living in Darkness Falls?"

Part of him was terrified to even drive through the urban landscape this late at night, which is why he was grateful Oscar stayed on the phone with him. Clive hoped Oscar would dispel the rumors, or at least bring them up, so he didn't have to ask.

"I dunno, but I needed to move out. You know that," Oscar paused for a second. "It's just a ton cheaper to rent an apartment here. People are terrified of this place, but I think it has some charm."

Clive thought of a lot of ways to describe Darkness Falls, but charm wasn't one of them. It wasn't the least bit charming to think that he was probably passing the same lone tree where a group of teenagers hanged themselves a few decades earlier. The story went that if you drove slowly under the tree, you could feel their feet scraping against the hood of your car.

There were so many other legends that Clive tried not to remember as he drove to Oscar's new place. Visitors told stories of having full conversations with people who were long dead. Others would hit someone with their car, but leave to see no one there and no damage to their vehicle.

Then there were cases of residents going missing, but nearby police usually suspected drug use or gang activity was involved. They refused to comment on any of the supernatural stories, but Clive sometimes wondered if they were afraid to spend too much time in Darkness Falls.

"I don't know Oz, it reminds me of something from a horror movie,' Clive chortled. 'But as long as it's close to work and you have your own space, I mean … you could save up and get a studio in New Springs or, where do your parents live again? Maybe you could–"

"Nah, nah, you don't really get it Clive. I would have to save up for at least a few years to afford a place in New Springs, based on my current salary. And I don't talk to my family at all anymore so … not all of us can do what you do …"

Clive opened his mouth to speak, but just pinched his lips for a second.

"… I'm sorry Clive, I know you were just trying to help. But I don't think I'm going anytime soon so, uh, I guess I just have to make the most of it here. I promise it's not that awful and I love horror movies, so …" he said with a laugh.

Clive paused again, before a familiar melody began playing on his radio and he turned the dial up.

"Oh my God, Oscar, I love this song! It's my phone alarm."

Sailors, fighting in the dance hall –

"Oh man! Look at those cavemen go! Come on, sing with me! Sing with me! *It's the freakiest shaaaoooowww!"*

Oscar laughed and belted out the last lyric with him.

Take a look at the lawman, beating on the wrong guy. Oh man, wonder if he'll ever know? He's in the best-selling shoooow. Is there life on Maaaaaars?

Clive and Oscar simultaneously took a breath as Bowie continued crooning. Clive daydreamed away from his driving and pictured the pop king in that music video, conjuring up the image of his baby blue eyeshadow and one pupil that was slightly larger than the other. For a second he was just lost in admiration for the celebrity who inspired him to come out of the closet when he was 15. He and his dad both loved Bowie.

But the film is a saddening bore. Because I've writ it ten times before. It's about to be writ again!

Clive renewed the conversation. "But Oz, I, uh, I was glad you asked me to visit you, especially if you needed company. I was excited to come. I'm almost at your place now and that took, like what, only 45 minutes."

"Yeah, uh, that's gonna be really cool Clive."

As I ask you to focus on —

Clive's heart leapt into his throat as he saw what appeared to be a homeless man standing on the road directly in front of him, he desperately swerved to avoid hitting him. As he maneuvered around the derelict he heard him yell "You can't be here." through the open window. Spinning the steering wheel in panic, Clive slammed against the corner of a sidewalk. He heard a dull pop as he pulled to the curb, checking quickly over his shoulder to make sure he didn't kill whoever was in the street. But whoever it was, they were gone.

"What was that?" Oscar asked, now from Clive's passenger seat as his phone flew from its resting place during the bump.

"There was somebody standing in the middle of the road and … shit. Shit, shit, shit, now I have a flat tire."

"Oh man, I'm sorry. Do you have a spare?"

"I think so. Don't laugh, but I, uh, I never changed a tire before. I know I'm missing a … that tool you need to twist each part into place. What's it called?"

Oscar laughed and, without missing a beat, said, "You should see if there's a gas station or something nearby where you could ask for help. I promise people here aren't as scary as this place makes it seem. What do you see around you?"

"Let me check. I'll call you back." And he hung up.

Clive saw an empty, graffiti-painted factory building to his right and a bodega to his left. Above the entrance was a dimmed neon sign blinking intermittently, which read, "24 Hours Convenience." There was a single gas pump to the left and a few scattered car parts stacked along the side of the building.

Clive walked inside and adjusted his eyes to the harsh fluorescent lighting. He surveyed rows of candy and cigarettes behind the counter. He dug his left hand in his coat pocket and lightly grazed the pepper spray, loosely closing his fingers around it.

"Hellooooo? Is anyone there?"

A gaunt and weathered-looking man in his forties stepped around another room and approached the counter. His hair was dark gray. He wore a dirt-stained blue chambray work shirt and khakis. As Clive spoke to him, he nodded with cold inquisition.

"Hey, uh, sir, I just popped my tire outside. I have a spare tire, but do you have the … uh …," Clive trailed off and reeled his hand to resemble the motion of –

His voice was gravely. "You need a lug wrench," the man said, matter-of-factly, as he started walking back toward the room he'd just appeared from. "Yeah, there's one in the room back here. Just give me a sec…"

Clive stood and waited, pursing his lips and bouncing on his heels. Then the man returned gripping what was definitely not a lug wrench. Clive felt desperately for his pepper spray as he saw the light bounce off of the pistol the man clutched in his hand.

"Easy now, easy. This ain't for you boy. I need your help," the stranger's voice cracked with the last sentence and he gently put the gun on the counter, slid it away from him and looked into Clive's eyes. Clive didn't know how old he was, but he somehow appeared to have aged ten years in that moment.

The man's voice went back to normal now and he spoke calmly, as if he was asking Clive for directions to the nearest mall.

"You don't look like you're from here … which is why I need you … I need you to pull the trigger. Please, I'm a Christian man – a good, God-fearing man – and I just want to see my mother and wife again. Please son."

He took the gun and held it out to Clive in his open palm as if it was a communion wafer. Now tears started to well up in his eyes as he pleaded for this twenty-something stranger to take his life.

You don't deserve for it to end like this Mike, he thought.

Clive stood there, struggling to find any words to say but he couldn't. His mind showed him a vignette of himself grabbing the gun and shooting the man in the head. His fingers tingled as he imagined gripping the metal in his hand. He was shaking and held his hands at his side defiantly when suddenly –

A phone on the wall behind the counter began to ring.

"Please son," Mike asked again, but Clive didn't budge. The phone continued to ring as they stood motionless. Mike knew that this wasn't going to work out as he planned. He nodded as a tear ran down his cheek and reluctantly put the gun back on the counter before picking up the phone.

His expression then snapped from one of anguish to absolute shock in a few wordless seconds and then he hung up the phone without saying a word.

Then, he turned back to Clive and his tone shifted into one of neighborly warmth as he pocketed the gun.

"Hey, let's get that tire of yours fixed. That sound good?"

Within twenty minutes, with Mike moving about his car with ease, Clive was back on his way with his headlights cutting through the pitch darkness as he headed to Oscar's apartment. He didn't even call his date because he wasn't quite sure how to explain what he just witnessed. Instead, he just texted that he was on his way and kept driving. He thought that maybe he hallucinated what happened, the whole experience.

But then as he looked sideways to make a turn he spotted something in his back seat. It caught his eye and made his heart leap into his chest. It was Mike's gun.

Oscar's apartment was on the first floor of a duplex with a tiny garage and inclined driveway. Most of the lots on the streets were like that and when Clive stared forward, he could make out the slim outline of taller factory buildings that made out the skeletal skyline of Darkness Falls.

When he turned back to Oscar's place, it was almost like an optical illusion. At first glance it looked clean, new and inviting. But the longer Clive looked, the dirtier and grayer its façade became. There was a busted window on the second floor. The garage door looked like someone tried driving a car through it.

However, as Clive looked at the rows of houses on each side, it didn't seem to stand out. Suddenly he was bothered that he'd pitched the idea of getting a studio apartment in New Springs. It would be the size of a cardboard box, but it would have to be better than this place.

He walked up to the front door. Oscar had answered his text.

Hey. Just come in. Sorry, I'm just in the shower. There should be beers in a fridge out in the garage if you want to grab a few for us. See you in a few minutes:)

Clive was surprised that the door wasn't locked but guessed that Oscar just left it open for him. *I hope he's usually more careful than this.* Clive walked inside and found the first inkling that he and Oscar would probably never want to live together. Oscar was a slob when he was on his own. But he'd never been like this before.

There were newspapers piled and scattered across the foyer. The walls were mostly bare, but the entire house looked like it needed a proper dusting. The smell of cigarettes clung to the air and masked an even more pungent odor that Clive couldn't quite distinguish, but reminded him of the sewage plant next to the playground near his home. He always mistook the strong odor of burning waste for some kind of flower because it had this sickly sweet undertone. He remembered the ripe stench always permeated the air during the start of spring. Clive absent-mindedly looked over a coffee table atop which sat an ashtray and a pile of weathered paperback novels.

He walked into the kitchen, where one busted lightbulb flickered ominously, and saw a half-eaten steak on the table with a baked potato and a glass of wine. Then he heard footsteps shuffle upstairs and decided to grab those beers for he and his date, although any appetite he once had was now dispelled by the turmoil.

There was a door in the back of the kitchen that led to the garage, and when Clive walked through the cigarette smell swiftly faded as the pungent scent of something bad overtook it. The off-white garage walls were streaked with rust-colored stains, dents and holes.

Inside the garage was an old station wagon, a work stool and a toolbox. But what was most perplexing were several black contractor bags piled next to each other.

Clive started for the fridge, but something in the back of his mind made him want to know what was in those contractor bags. Maybe it was just more newspapers or garbage, but did nobody collect trash in Darkness Falls? Maybe Oscar just became a bit of a hoarder.

He walked over to the bag on top of the pile and peaked into its opening, clutching the pepper spray in his pocket like a rosary. Succumbing to his curiosity, he withdrew his hand and slowly peeled open the contractor bag.

The plastic was slightly moist and that burning sewage smell intensified as he lifted it back. What he saw instantly made his hands grow clammy and his breath shorten.

The bag was stuffed with a rotting corpse. Oscar's rotting corpse.

Oscar's skin was purplish gray and dried blood was caked in his hair and on his clothes. His deep charcoal eyes stared straight ahead and his mouth hung open.

Clive was frozen. His hands started to shake violently as he shoved the bag away from him. His legs felt heavy and he thought that he would faint any second. He started dry-heaving and backed into the wall before sliding down and burying his face in his hands. But when he pulled them away, his friend's body was still there, the bag having slipped down, his eyes staring at the ceiling.

Oddly, he decided to take out his phone and tried calling Oscar. But after two rings –

Sorry, the number you have dialed is not in service.

Fuck. Fuck. FUCK. FUCK.

Clive tried to slow his breath and stop the panic attack that was already in full swing. Maybe if he closed his eyes hard enough, he would open them and the bag would just be full of days-old food. Then, he'd grab those beers, watch something on Netflix with Oscar and everything would be fine.

But like the mysterious encounter at the convenience store, this was no hallucination. He and Oscar had been talking for almost two months. Oscar wanted him to be here. But why?

Clive bit his lip so hard he almost drew blood, walked slowly over to the body bags and looked into Oscar's eyes. He was suddenly flooded with vivid memories of Oscar's old house – the Green Day poster, the cologne, the bowl ... but then Clive realized those weren't his memories. And he began to see flashes in the back of his mind of what happened almost two months earlier that led Oscar to Darkness Falls.

Oscar left his phone unattended on his kitchen table. That was mistake number one. His dad walked by just as Clive's fond goodnight text lit up the screen. When his parents confronted him with the phone open, Oscar first felt a wave of relief knowing he didn't have to bring it up himself. Maybe his parents would be on his side. But that relief soon turned to anger when they started screaming. They had the same bias as his brother.

"Think about how grandma would feel. You're her only grandson," his mom said.

So when his parents went to bed dejected and crying he left the house. He had no plans, no direction, not even a backpack. He didn't know where he was going or when he would come back, only that he refused to go back to his house. He left New Springs for good. Oscar spent hours walking aimlessly, he grew wary of his surroundings and decided to maybe turn around. But he only found himself going deeper and deeper into a blackness and realized he was completely lost in a new, ominous city that he never even knew existed.

Oscar kept walking and saw scenes in his peripheries that sent shivers down his back. Giant rats scurried in the streets, a group of teenagers in an alleyway were injecting themselves with God-only-knew-what and two homeless men were fighting over what appeared to be a sleeping bag. Then one screamed and Oscar snapped his head toward the scene to see blood pour down a fresh slice in the man's neck.

Oscar nearly jumped into the street before he heard a car's tires screech. He shook as he turned toward the driver, who he expected to be pointing a gun at his face, but instead he saw a warm expression from a middle-aged man with glasses and long brown hair.

"You look lost."

Clive tried calling the police, but his service kept fading in and out.

How fucking convenient.

He was suddenly out of the house and on his way back to his car, when he swung the door open and saw the gun sitting idly in the back seat.

Oscar wanted you to be here.

Within seconds, he was standing at the front door again with the gun nestled deep in his pocket. He didn't just walk in this time, he banged on the door five times and stood there hugging his sides as his mind flooded him with what seemed like a thousand different thoughts and scenarios. He imagined pulling the trigger as soon as the door opened, but knew it wouldn't be, couldn't be, that simple. So when the door did swing open he mumbled.

"Hi, sir? Sorry, I'm a bit lost."

His name was Lenny, or at least that's what he told Oscar as he drove him to his duplex, where he promised to make him dinner and drive him back the next day. Lenny said he lived on his own in Darkness Falls for the past five years, but grew up on Long Island with his family. His dad was in real estate, so he joined the family business and eventually broke off when he found Darkness Falls. It was the perfect place to fix up and modernize. There was so much free space that could easily be renovated with a little TLC. And the best part was that it was all so affordable.

Oscar had a hard time believing that anyone would want to live in this dark city. Part of him felt bad for Lenny. He didn't seem to have a spouse or kids. He was all on his own with some unattainable pipe dream in a nightmarish urban wasteland.

With no place to go Oscar decided to engage him and had dinner at his house. Maybe he could get some recommendations on where to stay, temporarily. He watched him make the food – mac and cheese to eat and ginger ale to drink. He still had one wary foot facing the door in case he'd need to leave in a hurry.

Typically, he would never have even gotten in a car with a stranger. He also wouldn't be walking on his own in a place like Darkness Falls. But his parents reaction unearthed the same depressive tendencies that led him to smoke his first joint behind the bleachers in high school when his brother called him a faggot for quitting football.

So Oscar sat there, smiling nonchalantly, as Lenny set the two bowls of food in front of them. The older man was going back for the drinks, when he stumbled and knocked the glasses onto the floor.

"Oh darn, I'm so sorry! I'm a bit clumsy and, well, accidents like this tend to happen a lot for me," he pulled out paper towels and began mopping up the soda, before Oscar decided it was only fair to help.

He didn't even notice when Lenny refilled the glasses, his back turned as he cleaned, or the few drops of GHB he added to Oscar glass. The last thing he remembered was tipping his head down into his cup and staring at the bubbles before …

Lenny invited Clive in, though he said he was expecting company any minute, and cleared a portion on the coffee table and insisted on making him a drink and hot soup before showing him directions out of Darkness Falls. He told him that he lived in town most of his life and worked as a night shift security guard at its only hospital.

Clive had a hard time believing any word that came out of Lenny's mouth. For all he knew, the guy could have rehearsed a different story for every lonely kid who ended up in those contractor bags.

"So what brought you to Darkness Falls?" Lenny asked, as he poured two drinks with his back turned. The microwave hummed with the soup inside that Clive had no intention of eating.

"I, um, I was meeting a friend here actually," Clive said. "But he, uh …"

Clive saw the slight of hand over his glass. "Hey, what did you just put in my drink?"

Lenny gripped the sides of the counter and Clive dug his hand into his pocket, gripping the pepper spray. But he relaxed his fingers when Lenny turned around and said –

"It's just ginger ale with lime. I always drink it that way."

"Oh I don't like limes, but thank you."

Lenny nodded, grinning anxiously, and turned back to the counter. The microwave beeped and Lenny made a grunt of approval before heading toward it. As he did, Clive slipped his hands into his pockets, gripped the gun in one hand, the pepper spray in the other, turning over several different ideas for his next move. Once he attacked, it would be a fight for his life. And he never even fired a gun. The pepper spray would give him enough time to make a break for it, but he wasn't trying to escape. He needed this man dead.

Oscar really should have found someone else for this.

… Oscar regained consciousness and found himself lying in a bed. His head throbbed and he looked up to see Lenny in the middle of fastening a handcuff around his wrist. Without thinking, he tugged as hard as he could and, luckily enough, caught Lenny by surprise. The handcuff wasn't locked yet, so Oscar broke free. He lunged off the bed before Lenny grabbed him from behind. But Oscar was stronger than him and slammed Lenny against the wall with his back. Then he ran down a staircase and out the door.

It took him all night but he made his way clear of Darkness Falls as tears streamed down his face in the cold wind. He was looking for any indication or sign pointing to the highway that led back to New Springs. He looked over his shoulder and saw Lenny's pickup truck gaining on him, so he turned down multiple side streets until he eventually saw what looked like a police station. Then he bolted inside.

He approached a startled officer who looked him over quizzically. The officer was wearing a New Springs Police Department uniform with a name tag that read *Matt Stockton*.

"I need … you …. to help me," Oscar stammered, catching his breath and fighting to find level ground. "Someone's trying … to kill me."

"Hold on, hold on boy, calm down. Where exactly are you coming from?"

"Darkness Falls," Oscar said and instantly regretted it as the officer seemed even more incredulous.

"Are you under the influence of alcohol or any drugs?" Matt asked.

"Someone brought me to his home there and drugged me –"

"So you are on drugs? What did you take?"

"I didn't take it … I was … was dosed with something. I don't know what happened next … but I woke up and … "

But then the door swung open and –

"There you are! I've been looking all over for you!"

– Oscar's heart dropped.

"That's him," he whispered, "That's him. Please help me," he pleaded hysterically to Officer Stockton.

"You'll have to forgive him, we had a big fight tonight and he ran from our apartment so upset. I'm sure he's been telling you all kinds of tall tales. I'm so sorry he inconvenienced you like this," Lenny said in his charismatic voice. And that was all it took.

What haunted Matt most about that interaction weren't the boy's gasps that turned to screams as the older man clasped a hand on his shoulder and led him out of the station insisting he not cause a scene. What hurt most was that part of Matt knew that he didn't try harder to protect the boy, but part of him didn't think any of it mattered. All he saw was another tweaker from Darkness Falls.

When the boy's mother called the station and reported Oscar missing, Matt was sick with dread that he had made the wrong call. And calls like that were not the kind you could easily turn back from. If a body turned up, the department would support his story. If surveillance video showed Oscar begging for help that night … then he better have one helluva an alibi.

So he decided to venture into Darkness Falls and see what he could find, despite the fact that he and his coworkers never went without a partner – let alone at night. He didn't know what he was looking for exactly. But when he saw the boy's familiar face, he jumped out of his car. He tried following Oscar and called out for him, but Oscar just took off. He chased Oscar around corners and through gutted buildings. He ran for what seemed like a half hour before Oscar finally turned around, revealing grayish skin and a torn open throat. Matt pinched his eyes shut and when he opened them, the boy was gone. So was the nightmare vision.

He spent the rest of the night driving around wanting to leave. But no matter how far Matt went in one direction, he ended up back in what seemed like the heart of the decaying urban hellscape. Was this some kind of twisted funhouse game, one with no end. Or did he have another agenda?

Lenny brought over two bowls of minestrone soup and placed them on the table and Clive's mind bounced back and forth between his ideas and anxieties. Lenny motioned for him to eat, but he wouldn't.

"C'mon, it's good. It'll get cold," Lenny said with a laugh, as he began eating some of his own. "So, uh, who's the friend you're meeting?"

Clive looked at the soup and took in the aroma, but no matter how much he focused on it, he still couldn't get that smell out of his nose. The smell of –

"You might know him," Clive said and closed his fingers around the pepper spray in his pocket. "His name… is Oscar."

Lenny furrowed his brow before Clive saw the sudden realization cross the killer's face. The next series of events happened so fast that Clive could hardly remember them, but at the same time they felt like slow motion.

Clive pulled the pepper spray from his pocket and Lenny lunged across the table to knock it out of his hand, but not before Clive twisted the cap and slammed his finger down.

"AAAGGHHHAAAYYY'LLLL KUH-KUH-KILL YOOOOUUUU!"

He stumbled backwards before bolting forward and pushing the table into Clive's chest. Clive dodged him and ran to his left and into the garage. He slammed the door closed and wedged a nearby work stool under it. Lenny started slamming his fists against the door and violently turning the knob.

Clive immediately took out his phone again, praying he would have service so that he could call the police. But there was nothing.

When he looked up, Oscar was standing next to him, a ghostly apparition with a grave expression. Next to Oscar was another boy in his early twenties and to his right was another boy.

They gathered around Clive, who took a deep breath, pulled the gun out of his pocket and held it shakily in front of him. They all ushered him forward like parents assisting a child to take his first steps and Clive did. Then he kicked the stool out from under the doorknob.

He waited a split second for it to swing open, then pulled the trigger.

Clive's vision turned into a red haze, then went dark.

He thought he had fainted, but when he opened his eyes he was in his bedroom 30 miles away from Darkness Falls. Despite feeling Lenny's blood spray against his face, he was completely dry. He slowly started gauging his surroundings as David Bowie's voice crooned from his phone alarm. *He's in the best selling shoooooooooow.*

Then he grabbed his phone and searched Oscar's name in Google. The first result to pop up linked to an article from that same morning.

Suspected serial killer found dead in Darkness Falls

A man police are now calling the Demon of Darkness Falls has been found dead in his apartment by a New Springs police officer after there were reports of a gunshot. At least three dismembered bodies were discovered in contractor bags in 52-year-old Lenny Greyson's garage, where he appears to have died from a self-inflicted gunshot wound.

One of the bodies has been identified as belonging to missing 25-year-old Oscar Mendez, whose mother said he left his family home about two months ago. Recently released surveillance footage from the New Springs Police Department shows Mendez running into the offices of the 72nd Precinct, followed by Greyson, that same night his mother said he went missing.

In the footage, Mendez pleads for help from Officer Matt Stockton – who is the same cop that found Greyson's body. It is not yet clear what led Stockton to Greyson's house and he has yet to comment on the footage.

Meanwhile, Mendez's mother Sarah has provided us with this statement from the family:

"We're so, so relieved to have some closure in finding out what happened to our son. Oscar was a beautiful, sensitive and caring boy."

Clive stopped reading for a second, overwhelmed by a thousand different feelings and struggling to figure out what he actually went through in the past 24 hours. What had he done? How had he come out of the darkness? He looked back at the article.

"We're grateful for the police who found out what happened. As for the footage, I know Oscar would forgive Officer Stockton, knowing that at least the killer can't hurt anyone else."

Just then, Clive's phone buzzed. It was Oscar's number.

His text included a screenshot of that last line and after it, simply read:

"Would I though?"

Clive shut down his phone, the screen going dark.

PETE'S PLACE

WILLIAM JOHN ROSTRON

The marker on the side of the highway read, "Darkness Falls – 2 miles." This told me that there was a destination on this road—a direction. This sign provided some comfort because where I had come from remained a mystery to me. I remember very little about my past, and my definition of "past" is any event longer than three minutes ago. It was as if I had just been plucked from somewhere unknown and placed in this car on this road.

I knew that my name was Isaac from an ornamental ID bracelet that I wore on my wrist. I believe that I am eighteen years old (I am not positive of this because I can't recall seventeen years, three hundred sixty-four days, twenty-three hours, and fifty-seven minutes of that time.). I knew that I had never seen the car I was now driving and probably could not even describe its exterior. I knew there was an old guitar case in the back seat and that I had memories of playing that instrument. However, any information beyond those facts eludes me.

As the two miles elapsed, I came to realize that the "exit" for Darkness Falls was not an exit—the entire road proceeded in that direction and that direction alone. Therefore, I had no choice but to move toward what I thought was a town. But maybe Darkness Falls was a reference to a waterfall, like Niagara Falls. I didn't know that either.

As the road curved to the right, visibility became impossible. It was oppressively dark, even though only moments ago the sun had shined brightly. I proceeded cautiously, with the car's headlights barely showing the immediate ten feet in front. I did this for what seemed like hours, but the clock on my dashboard only registered a few minutes. Then, I perceived brightness in the distance and drove toward it. When I reached the end of the dark (the darkness that fell?), I was stunned.

I don't know the technical term for what I was seeing. This area was the opposite of a plateau—an almost perfectly flat circular surface a thousand feet lower than the rim upon which I now rested. somewhat like a crater. The singular path down to the bottom was this road I was on. I then began to see a town.

As I drove by a large sign that read Darkness Falls, I could see an elaborate system of side streets that all branched off from one main thoroughfare that was dead center in the town. Someone had a sense of humor in naming this extra-wide paved boulevard as "Earth Avenue."

I drove patiently, taking in the unusual sights around me. The road down the middle of town had three lanes with angled parking on each side. One lane went in each direction of the town, which was not uncommon. However, the lane in the middle went *only* into town. Giant arrows painted every ten feet told the driver to move forward. I would have thought this was some express lane for quick travel through the municipality, except that I could see in the distance that remaining on this path would take me right into the rock wall that made up the end of the valley. It was like the road was telling me, *go forward until you decide where to get off, but you must get off.*

There didn't seem to be any question about which side of the road to park. As I had slowly traversed the town, a distinct pattern emerged. The left side of the road was depressing. The buildings were a ramshackle combination of poorly built and decaying structures. Indeed, from what I could see, even the people I passed seemed despondent and morose. They rambled onward, not seeming to be in any rush to arrive at any location. A gray hue hung over that side of the boulevard. This haze obstructed my ability to see what was going on with any great accuracy.

Meanwhile, the right side of the road seemed to be painted in brilliant colors, with every detail of its buildings in perfect condition. There did not seem to be many people populating this side. However, those who were there displayed bright, engaging smiles. I moved from the center lane to the right lane and stopped a young man walking briskly down the street. He appeared to be someone right out of the 1950s, with greased-back curly blonde hair. However, he had a broad, friendly smile as he came over to my car and looked in.

"Where can I get something to eat and drink in this town," I questioned.

He looked me over intensely, and then his eyes spotted the guitar case in the rear seat.

"You probably should be heading over to Pete's Place. It's just down the road. I think that you'll like it there. Good food and drink… and a whole lot shakin' goin' on…you know, music…real good music."

So, I took the guy's advice and soon found myself standing under a sign that read, "Pete's Place – A Beautiful Club Experience." *A weird description*, I thought. The building only had a thirty-foot, one-story exterior, so I didn't expect much. However, I was beginning to feel that I had gone insane when I passed through the front door and found myself in a vast concert hall—a much bigger space than the exterior implied.

There were three stages—one on each side and one on the rear wall. The place seemed filled, but as soon as I started to look for a place to sit, a table and chair became available right in front of me. I was starving, but no one came to my table. I felt frustrated as my hunger grew and finally stopped a passing patron.

"Is the service here always this bad," I complained.

He laughed. "You're new here."

"Yeah, just walked in the door."

"What would you like?"

"Why, are you the waiter?" He laughed at me again but apologized when he saw I was getting annoyed.

"I'm sorry. I forgot what it was like my first time here. Just think about what you would like, and you'll soon be taken care of."

"How do I know they have what I want?"

"They'll have what you want. So don't worry about anything. It will be taken care of."

"By you? Just tell me because I need to hit the head?"

"It's over there," he said and pointed over to a corner.

When I had finished my business, I returned to the table. Sitting right in front of me was exactly what I had been thinking of...a well-done burger with melted cheddar cheese, bacon, and just the right amount of ketchup. Next to it were seasoned curly fries and an Arnold Palmer drink. What the heck?

When I looked over a few tables, the guy I talked to gave me a thumbs up. I had never said what I wanted to anyone. I should have questioned this whole series of events but didn't. I was too hungry. Besides, one of the stages had just come to life.

A young guy who looked like a young Chuck Berry was playing the guitar as beautifully as the original had. He even had his stage moves down as he crushed a version of "Roll Over Beethoven." He followed with a whole set of Berry's songs that were so good that I almost forgot how delicious my hamburger was.

When he finished his short set, the stage went dark, and to my surprise, another location lit up almost immediately. It was then that I realized that this club was set up as a place for tribute bands to hone their craft. The guy on this stage was doing Jim Croce material exceptionally well. I listened as he artfully performed "Operator," "Leroy Brown," and "Time in a Bottle." Then that stage went blank, and the stage to my left became active.

I had always longed to be at a Chris Delaney and the Brotherhood Blues Band concert, but they were gone before my time. However, these guys were doing their hit, "Dancing on the Other Side of the Wind," just as I expected it would have sounded live from the originals. By now, I had finished my meal and ambled over to a crowd of people who were following the music from stage to stage. We now found ourselves at the first stage again.

"Those Born Free? I never heard of them." I questioned, and one of the girls answered.

"Not all great bands made it or were famous. However, here we don't differentiate. Good music is good music…and good bands are good bands." She winked and then added something I didn't understand, "Good in every sense of the word."

And they were good, and so were the three bands that followed that I had never heard of but enjoyed immensely. I forgot where I was and that I had no memory of anything before driving on the road toward Darkness Falls…and I amazingly didn't care. The hours flew by, and I had a great time and worried about nothing.

I soon found out that the definition of good music was not limited to rock. At times two of the stages were active, and by some miracle of acoustics, their sounds did not clash. If you were near one stage, you heard the music being played there, and if you drifted over to the other stage, that was the only sound you heard. The group of people I had started to hang with decided to educate me on different genres and expand my musical interests. I stood enchanted by some great jazz—a style I had never really given a chance. I then was introduced to a big band ensemble that they told me was Benny Goodman's style. I even listened to some Indian Bollywood stuff followed by some mariachi from Mexico.

Perhaps, the most unusual style for my tastes was sitar music. I knew it was popular in the 1960s when the Beatles "discovered" Ravi Shankar in India and brought him back to the United Kingdom. They even used the instrument on some of their albums. But, as I stood appreciating the performance, one of the guys, I think his name was Johnny, started a conversation that made no sense to me.

"I sure hope we get to hear one or both of his daughters play here," declared Johnny excitedly. His girlfriend, Maria, sharply answered him.

"Why would you wish that? Sometimes, I think your head is up to your…"

"It's okay, Maria. I don't think he meant it that way. No one here would mean it that way," chuckled a friend of theirs called Gio.

Now I was baffled and had no idea what that conversation was even about. I was about to make that point when another one of their friends named Jimmy Mac called us over to another stage.

"Smokey Joe is about to perform," Jimmy Mac was screaming to his friends. Talk about confusion. I was a big fan of Mississippi Delta Blues. My mentor, Southy Sam Layton, had told me stories of the 1930s blues greats and had had me listen to some of the old records that he had. But, wait! I just realized that I remember something from my past. Southy Sam Layton had taught me to play the guitar from when I was ten years old to...? That I can't remember. I only know that he taught me well, and I spent many years with him. It didn't matter to either of us that Sam was white, and I was black. He knew the blues as well as if he had been there himself. He told me that he had learned everything about the guitar and life from an old black man named Fast Jesse.

In the waning years of his life, Fast Jesse had taken the young Sam under his wing and made him a professional musician who went on to fame and fortune. The famous Southy Sam Layton had then returned to my little section of town to live out his final years. Besides using the wealth he had accumulated to help the poor of Southy, he taught me everything he knew. Included in that was the story of Smokey Joe. So now there was a young guy, perhaps in his late twenties, ready to do a tribute to this great but never famous blues musician.

If the *real* Smokey Joe Watson was half as good as his imitator, he should have been famous. He should have been rich and not have died penniless and alone as Fast Jesse said he did. But, instead, I listened to this "Smokey Joe" bend the strings and run his fingers over the frets with a skill that I could only dream of achieving. I stood entranced as his half-hour of playing time held me mesmerized.

When he was done, I turned to my friends and asked what his name was. The group of Johnny, Jimmy Mac, Maria, and Gio were moving away from me.

"Sorry, we're on soon. Gotta go," yelled Johnny through the crowd and then realized that they were the band Those Born Free that I had heard playing earlier.

"But what's his name?"

"Joe," I thought I heard from Gio as he laughed.

Then right behind me, I heard a voice.

"Smokey Joe Watson is my name, and I hear you is Isaac," spoke the young black man who had just been on the stage.

"No, what's your name really?"

"My momma done name me Joseph Watson, but that quickly become Joe. When I got older and developed a taste for tobacco, I soon became Smokey Joe."

"Cut the crap," I answered just a bit too quickly.

"You have no idea where you are or what's going on…do you?"

I didn't answer.

"I guess that's why my friends picked me to tell you the truth of the matter."

"What's that?"

"Let's talk outside…I need a smoke."

Now I thought he was just staying in character—you know, the whole "Smokey" Joe Watson image. However, when we got outside, he lit up an unfiltered Camel. He was committed to the character. I played along.

"Those things will kill you," I warned, and I have never heard somebody laugh so loud. Apparently, I had said something funny.

"Robert Johnson used to say that to me."

Now I had him. Here is this twenty-something telling me that he knew *the* Robert Johnson, the greatest blues guitarist of all time. However, Johnson had died in the 1930s. To be honest, I could not remember what year I was living at that moment, but I did remember that it was the 21st century. I also knew how to catch "Smokey Joe" in his lie.

My teacher and mentor, Southy Sam, had told me the true story of Robert Johnson. It had been passed on to him by his teacher/mentor Fast Jesse, a friend and contemporary of Robert Johnson. It was a story only the four of us knew. I would test this Smokey Joe wanna-be.

"Tell me the story," I insisted.

Smokey Joe took one final drag on his unfiltered cigarette, crushed it out on the floor, and began.

❦

Robert Johnson and I played all the juke joints in the South during the 1930s. I was pretty good, but he was the best. That weren't always so. At first, he was just an okay kind of player and singer. He wasn't happy with that, so he did something that I would never do—he went down to the Crossroads. Now we all knew who he would meet at those crossroads. But the rest of us never dared go there. Robert did.

He give his guitar to the devil, and when the devil give it back...well... Robert become the best guitar picker and singer of all. However, he paid a price—his soul.

"I know that legend. Many, many people do. It has been written about endlessly, and it makes a good story. However, only the real Smokey Joe would know the rest of the tale...the part he passed on to Fast Jesse, and that Fast Jesse passed on to Southy Sam who then passed on to me. If you are really Smokey Joe, then you know what I am talking about."

"You mean about his last night on Earth and what he done told me? I guess you is testin' me."

"Yes, I am. Only the real Smokey Joe would know," I challenged him quite skeptically.

"Okay, you asked for it."

So me and Robert are sittin' the bar takin' a break from playing. He suddenly takes my hand and says, "I just want to say goodbye." I ask him what he means, and he just puts up his hand up to stop me from talkin'.

"Let me tell you my story. I went down to the crossroads, and the devil give me all the skill in the whole wide world for the price of my soul."

"I knows that," I interrupt.

"No, Smokey, you and everyone else suspect that much, but you didn't know...at least not for sure. No, I'm telling you it's the truth, and I can't even say 'so help me God' because I give up that right after I made my deal."

"We been friends for a long time," I say to him. "Why you be tellin' me this now?"

"Because that devil man be a tricky son-of-a-bitch. There be a part of the

deal that no one know about but me. See, when he makes the deal, he seal it with a tattoo that appear on my stomach. It's small—with just the number 333 right at my waist. It was his symbol for those he owned. His sign in the good book is 666, so those he own is 333.

"So what?" I ask him.

"So, I figure it's a ciphering thing. 3 time 3 time 3. That be 27—the age the devil man come for me.

My friend Robert died the next day…at age 27.

"Holy Shit, that was the story I knew, but how could you know?" I thought to myself; *The real Smoky Joe would be way over a hundred years old!"* From his answer, I realized that he could read my mind. He answered my unspoken question.

"You stop counting years…when the darkness falls."

"Darkness falls, you mean that's just not the name of this town it's…"

"Would like it better if the town was called…Kicked the bucket…Pushing up daisies…or…Taking a dirt nap?"

"You mean…"

"Yes, I do. Not only that, but the big man up there has a sense of humor. He be makin' fun of all those poor souls like Robert who made a deal the devil. You see, all of us here in Pete's Place are in our '27-year-old bodies.' It's kinda nice."

"But then what is this place…exactly?" I was confused.

"I think it's pretty clear from the name." He pointed up toward the sign which read, "Pete's Place."

"Yeah, he likes to be called Pete…a bit less snobby than St.…you know."

I then looked up at the bottom sign that I had read as "A Beautiful Club Experience" during the daylight. However, I now saw that many of the letters were not lit up. The neon "u" was dulled. Half of the second "u" was gone, as was the "l." Only the "C" of club appeared. The result was "*A Bea tifi C Experience*—A Beatific Experience."

I was having a hard time taking all this in when I remembered the rest of the Robert Johnson story. So many of the young music superstars had met a similar fate, dying at the same age. The media had sarcastically dubbed them the "27 Club"… Janis Joplin, Jimi Hendrix, Jim Morrison, Brian Jones, Amy Winehouse, Kurt Cobain—those are just ones the world knew. Had they gone down to the crossroads and made similar deals with the devil?

I forgot Smokey Joe could read my mind. He pointed across the street. It was the first time I recalled the drive into town that afternoon. I flashed back to the split in the road and how the two sides of "Earth Avenue" were so different. Now, as I looked over to the other side of the boulevard, the haze began to clear, and I could see the dilapidated buildings, devoid of color or life. I could hear music coming out of one decrepit storefront. It was not exactly music in that it was so out of tune that it hurt my ears to listen to it. I then looked at the sign that appeared next to the door. I understood all that was to be understood.

Appearing Tonight
Janis Joplin with The Doors
Tomorrow Night
Jimi Hendrix with his special guest Robert Johnson

Just when I thought I had taken all this in, Smokey Joe pointed to the sign above the front door of that venue. My eyes followed his finger until they rested on the name of the club, "Highway to Hell."

"Seen enough?" Smokey Joe uttered as he guided me back into Pete's Place.

"Is this some kind of entry place or something?"

"Yes and No. We all enter here to…well, you know where…but we are also free to come back and visit whenever we feel like it. So many of us do that a lot."

It's funny how I almost didn't notice that Smokey Joe had lost the unique backwoods drawl that he had spoken with earlier. Again reading my mind, he shrugged his shoulders at my thought.

"Here you can be whatever you want to be…and you don't have to pay for it with your soul."

I guess I understood even though I was only eighteen and had hardly lived. Smokey Joe again read my mind.

"Wait here a second," he ordered. He didn't explain but went to my car and took out my guitar case. Together we reentered the club.

As I stood in the doorway, the entire club stood and cheered as if they had been waiting for me all day. The applause continued while I was led to the stage. I reached to take my guitar case from Smokey Joe, but he held it firm while someone came up from the side with a guitar in each hand.

"Would you prefer a Fender Stratocaster or a Gibson Les Paul?"

I grabbed the Strat as Smokey Joe walked off the stage clutching my guitar case, all the while smiling at me. Meanwhile, I found myself surrounded by a full band that looked like they knew what they were doing. Of course, they all looked 27 years old.

I was especially curious about the two guitarists who appeared on either side of me. They seemed vaguely familiar. One was black, and one was white. However, I was so excited that I didn't think much of it. My memory of music returned rapidly, and I played like I was possessed (wrong choice of words in this location?).

I played some Clapton and some Mississippi Delta blues that Southy Sam, my mentor, had taught me. I even remember playing a few songs that I remember writing and performing (and perhaps recording). But how did these two guitarists know these songs? They even took solos harmonically tuned to the solos that I was taking. This might have been the greatest moment of my life...or was it now afterlife?

When I was done, I received thunderous applause. Sorry, no humility here--not after that moment. The two guitarists and I went and sat at a table. I had to know more about them. Smokey Joe joined us.

"How did you know what I was going to play?" I asked them.

"Hell, I might have taught you some that," the white guy answered but did not elaborate.

"Jesse, why don't you explain. This kid is confused."

"Okay, here's the scoop. Me and Smokey Joe grow up together and was good friends—my best friend. The night before he passed away, he give me his guitar. He says, 'I gotta go, you take this.' Then he says, "You remember three things in life: 'You pray to God, you be good to your momma, and you take care of this guitar.' You have to under-stand that our mommas had also been good friends, but they had long since passed away. But we would always say to each other. 'Be good to your momma,' which meant be good to *all* people."

"And I did remember," whispered Jesse. "Yup, right until I give away the guitar to this young man," he chuckled as he slapped the young blonde sitting next to him on the shoulder. "I figure giving it to him was my way of taking care of it."

Fast Jesse looked at Smoky Joe and smiled, "We're looking good now, right?"

The two of them appeared as healthy, vibrant 27-year-olds, laughing and enjoying life, or should I say the afterlife. But as I glimpsed once again at them for one brief moment, I saw Smokey Joe and Fast Jesse as the old men they must have been when he passed away. My face must have given away my shock.

"From the look you are giving me, you must have seen our 'old selves." We do that every so often to remember how lucky we are. You'll see," commented Smokey Joe. However, Fast Jesse seemed impatient to continue the story.

"I didn't live that much longer after Smokey left me, but damn I played the best guitar of my life. But I don't think it was just me. I felt that every time I played, my buddy was right there beside me...or better yet, in me. He was helping me to be better in every way."

"Just like a ghost in your guitar?" I blurted out. I don't know where I got that phrase or what it meant. I just knew it. I had heard it. I had lived it!

"Yes, that's just what it was like," recalled Fast Jesse.

Almost like a vision, I again saw Fast Jesse as an ancient guitarist. He was in a dilapidated old house, and he was with a young blonde guitarist who appeared to be around the age of 17. The Fast Jesse in my vision was at the end of the road. He spoke in a broken, failing voice that struggled to remember the exact words that had been said to him years before by Smokey Joe. He handed the young boy the guitar.

"I gotta go. You take this," uttered the rasping voice to the young blonde. I could see the faint image of Smokey Joe standing behind his friend Jesse, whispering in his ear.

"You remember three things: You pray to God. You be good to your momma, And you take care of this guitar."

The vision then transformed into a scene of this young boy playing to a large crowd of adoring fans. Over his shoulder, I could see Fast Jesse smiling, almost urging on the performance…helping the young man play…just like the ghost in his guitar. But how did I know that phrase? And then the young man began to age before my eyes, and I understood. Southy Sam Layton, my teacher, mentor, and friend, was indeed the young man sitting at the table with me. He smiled at me when he knew I finally understood. As tears rolled down my eyes, I hugged him with all my might. Memories returned to me of a few days ago when he had left me as a man well into his eighties. And then I mouthed the words he had said to me.

"I gotta go. You take this. You remember three things: You pray to God. You be good to your momma. You take care of this guitar."

I didn't see it then, but I now knew that Smokey Joe and Fast Jesse must have been looking over Southy Sam's shoulder.

I looked back at the three guitarists who now had all returned to their youthful appearances. Southy Sam smiled, and our reunion was only broken by the words of Smokey Joe.

"It's time," was all he said and handed me my guitar case. I held it in my hands, realizing that this guitar had been played by all three of them, and whenever I lifted it in my arms, they would be with me. I couldn't wait to retake the stage. I placed the case on a table, unlocked the three latches, and lifted the cover.

The case was empty.

I looked at the three of them, and they simply smiled at me, saying nothing.

Memories of my life flooded back into my consciousness. I was twenty and playing on stage, and the crowd was cheering—Southy Sam's vision stood behind me, guiding me.

And then I was thirty-something, and the crowds were more significant, and they were singing along to my songs as if they had heard recorded versions. I felt the admiration of fans, and more importantly, the love of friends and family as the scenes rapidly changed.

My life progressed through all its beautiful moments—maybe some not so wonderful as I watched my wife pass away from cancer in her sixties. I was alone.

"Oh, she's here," uttered Southy Sam. "She just wanted you to understand this whole thing before she came down the stairway from…well, you know where."

I couldn't wait. I remembered how lonely I had been at the end… until I met a boy named Jake. I took the twelve-year under my wing and taught him the guitar, and his family became my family in my final years.

And then I knew why the guitar was not in its case. It had never been in there while I was riding on the way to Darkness Falls. Instead, I had followed the tradition laid down by Smokey Joe, Fast Jesse, and Southy Sam. And in my last act on the planet, I had told the young man…

"I gotta go. You take this. You remember three things: You pray to God. You be good to your momma. And you take care of this guitar."

And then…I had given the guitar to Jake.

STRANGE FATE

HENRY VINICIO VALERIO MADRIZ

The sound of the flames drilled Miles' ears and alerted his senses. He looked at his right, then at his left: all the room was burning and soon the whole building would be burning down. He had no idea how the fire started, something flammable must have broken in the struggle. It was time to leave. Besides, somebody could find him there and the truth would be discovered. The doctor's hacked corpse stayed in a strange position… it looked like he was trying to run away, what an irony! Miles picked up his ax.

"You fought well but couldn't escape from me, old man!" Miles said. His wrath was gone. However, he was not content at all with what he had just done. He left the clinic. The fire lit his way.

Miles went home to tell Stella, his wife and the only star in this dark sky, how he got revenge for her. His wife probably would calm him down. Stella was the only person who was able to control Miles' tempestuous temper, everybody knew that.

"It's done! And I don't regret it… AT ALL! He'll never rape you, or anyone else, ever again… I didn't like you working as a janitor there anyway," Miles gestured as he cleaned his lumberjack's ax with rags.

Stella broke down and started sobbing. "I would have never told you about this disgrace if a baby hadn't been growing in my belly. A child that is not yours."

"He will be mine now. Ours." Miles said with certainty.

"But how can it be? Don't you see it, Miles? The police will find it out, and you'll be put in jail… don't you understand it? They'll come here to question both of us. We'll probably both get arrested. You must go away, for a while, until things return to normal."

Miles stowed his ax in the shed, put some personal care products and some clothes into a backpack, kissed his wife on her forehead, and left without saying another word. He didn't know where to go and he had just that night to figure it out.

As Miles wandered out of Darkness Falls, he was able to see the light of the fire. The clinic was still burning, and the heroic firefighters were doing their noble job. Fire seemed to be the only light that ever flourished in this town. He wondered why he and Stella had stayed there for so long when all their friends had left long ago. It was a lonely place with an appropriate name. When he came back, he would take Stella and go far away.

Without noticing what direction, he was going he traveled for days, mostly on foot, sometimes hitching a ride. Miles stopped when he saw the ocean, standing on the loading docks staring into the vastness of the sea. Consequently, he thought if he had to be gone, what better idea than to join a cargo ship. He saw a man who looked like he might be a ship officer headed toward a vessel. A big guy with a big gut in a fisherman's sweater and boots.

"Hey, sir! Sir!"

The man noticed Miles and stopped.

"Excuse me, sir. Are you part of the crew of this freighter?"

"Sure, am. I'm the captain," the man answered back.

"Captain, do you need extra men on your boat? I can be very helpful… I'm a strong guy and a good worker," Miles said.

"My SHIP, you meant…"

"Yes sir, that's what I meant."

"As a matter of fact, I'm missing a man, turned sick this afternoon… This is not our regular policy to hire new personnel without references, but as I'm in a bind I guess I'll make an exception this time! Come on aboard."

Miles had been lucky. Even though he had never been on a freighter before he adapted well to the routine and learned fast. Working on a ship somehow came natural for him. He pondered if he should give up his profession as a lumberjack. It was never really the job for him but he had stumbled into that job years ago almost as oddly as he'd fallen into this one. After a few weeks, he had adjusted to sea life and was able to do his job as efficiently as the regular crew. He worked hard everyday but thought fondly of Stella and wondered how long he would have to stay away. He'd miss a lot of things.

Miles had worked for months when Hunter joined the ship's crew. They were in port for a day to load up on supplies and take on new cargo when he came aboard.

"Hunter, this is Miles, and although he's a rookie, he'll teach you as good as anyone on the ship and he'll show you around, right," the captain barked.

"Yes, sir!"

"So, you are Miles?" Hunter asked as soon as the captain left.

"Yeah, I am; why?"

"No, nothing…"

Hunter noticed Miles' interrogative face, therefore, he tried to adjust his last words. "I've heard a lot about your excellent work… that's all."

"Yeah, well we'll see what kind of seaman you'll make," Miles expressed, just a little unsure of the newcomer.

Hunter felt released.

Days passed and Hunter seemed to look for any chance to talk to Miles, asking probing conversations.

"Hey Miles, tell me, are you from here?"

"Yeah… not really. I'm from a city that's inland but I prefer to live here and to stay on the ship."

"I understand. Sometimes we have nothing left at home, right?" Hunter added.

"Actually, I used to have a wife over there…" Miles didn't understand why he opened up, revealing Hunter his secret. He'd never told anyone else.

"Really! You divorced her?"

Miles kept silent, coiling the long line of rope he was working on.

"Yeah. I know, women can be complicated sometimes… like this woman I know about from Darkness Falls… Ah but never mind. You don't want to hear that story."

Miles was intrigued but leery at the same time and let it drop. A couple of days later though he approached Hunter while off duty and questioned him.

"You talked about Darkness Falls. I'm from that area. What's happening over there?"

Hunter finished chewing his sandwich and gladly shared his news.

"Do you remember the clinic that was there? The one that burned down."

"Sure…, yeah, I mean I heard about it. Did they figure out anything?"

"Plenty."

Now Miles was fascinated that Hunter knew about the story, and he eagerly wanted to hear if it had been solved or it blew over.

"Well, there's this woman, I think her name is Stella, and she worked there. She was having a romance with the doctor's son while her husband was away, breaking his ass working as a lumberjack. The clinic had some economic problems, you know, the old man… had two mortgages on the place because he needed some money to cover his son's university studies and some other whims this young buck had, you know, wine, girls, the whole shebang… you know what I mean. The thing was that the poor doctor had several debts to pay, and the clinic was not turning a profit anymore. Nothing in Darkness Falls was. So, and this is the good part, the doctor's son convinced his lover, Stella, to tell her husband that the old doctor raped her; for her to explain how she got pregnant while her husband was away," Hunter was interrupted by Miles.

"Shit! I mean, damn that's interesting…"

"Sure is. What happened next you might have already guessed it! The dumb bastard got enraged and killed the good doctor and ran away. While defending himself, the doctor must have accidentally started the fire. Lucky loving pigeons got away with it all."

"Lucky?" Miles interrupted again.

"Don't you see it? The clinic was no longer worth it to run but the doctor's son got all of the money from the insurance. Now the two love birds are enjoying their new nest, with a new kid and a lot of extra commodities... The woman's husband made all that dream come true! Now he's running from the law and she's the one with all the dough. Funny story, huh?" Hunter finished his narrative.

Miles said nothing for a while. Then he thought he was supposed to react somehow...

"You're right. Some people are born to live a bitter life."

"You bet. Well, let's get back to work or the captain will fire us", Hunter said.

Miles couldn't stop thinking about Hunter's story. It was his story. And it ate into his guts like shipboard rats.

A month later, the next time the ship docked into port, Miles asked the captain for some time off and went to visit his wife for some payback.

When he arrived in Darkness Falls a day later the first place he went to was the shed for his ax. Miles banged in through the front door and his wife was shocked to see him.

"Stella?"

"Miles!"

"What are you doing here?"

"I know it all," he spit out as he swung the ax and planted the blade into the wood cabinet next to Stella's head.

Miles didn't let his wife say another word and took her by her neck with both strong hands. Without stopping Miles squeezed her throat until she was gasping, then blue then convulsing and finally motionless. No tears rolled down his cheeks as her eyes bulged from their sockets, now sightless, and she went down. He yanked the handle from the wood and sized up the best way to chop her up. Suddenly, flashing colored lights and the sound of sirens announced that the Darkness Falls police had arrived. Stunned Miles went to the window.

"Hands up and come out of the house", a police officer ordered.

'How did they know?' Miles wondered, but he offered no resistance.

Miles was hand-cuffed and read his rights. While he was escorted to the police patrol car, he thought he saw the dark image of a familiar man outside his house.

The trial didn't take long. Miles was defeated and confessed to both murders. He was sentenced to double life imprisonment at Shapak Prison, the facility on the hill that overlooked Darkness Falls.

"Miles, you got some new company," the prison officer said.

"What about Lizard?"

"Lizard? Lizard is not sharing this cell anymore… he was killed yesterday, didn't you hear?"

"Well, I knew someone stabbed him, but I didn't know he died", Miles protested.

"This is Thomas", the prison officer introduced the new inmate and left.

"Everybody calls me Tomahawk", the prisoner explained and reached to shake hands.

"I'm Miles."

After the officer was out of earshot Tomahawk dared to ask Miles a personal question.

"Are you THE Miles who worked as a lumberjack and on a cargo ship? Killed his wife?"

"Yeeesss…"

"Was your wife's name Stella?"

"Yeah, but how do you know?

"What are you about, pal? Speak up." Miles said, annoyed.

"Relax man. It's just… it's just that I have to tell you a story."

Miles remembered the last time someone said that to him and how it ended up… another man, another story. He began to really hate stories.

"Ok, Tomahawk. You have my attention. I'm all ears," his words thick with sarcasm.

"Listen, I got arrested because I worked for a guy; kind of work only certain individuals want to do…if you catch my meaning. And in the end, the bastard set me up. And here I am."

"That's a great story, what does it have to do with me?" Miles asked with waning interest.

"That's not the story. You see, this guy used to tell me he got rich by banging a pretty chick… her name was Stella… your wife, I believe. Man, you have my respect, don't get me wrong, I'm just telling you what I heard, ok?"

"Ok. Keep going."

"The man was always bragging about how astute he was because he found a beautiful married woman who satisfied him while her husband was working in the mountains. The man said she was crazy about him. But she got pregnant and wanted to keep it, so they both needed a way out. So, they came up with the idea that the guy's father had raped her. An old man. Can you believe it? Sorry man, I realize you know that part of the story. They made you believe that the doctor raped her because, on one hand, your wife assured him you were an aggressive man who would probably kill the doctor, on the other hand, the guy wanted the father dead. This way he would be able to maybe sell the clinic to get some money even though the clinic had mortgages. But things got crazy, you know after the murder and the fire, and the doctor's son wound up getting the insurance money when the clinic burned."

"I know that story… you're not telling anything new. I went to jail for it. A crew member told me the same thing. It seems to me that everybody knows my story", Miles regretted.

"Was the crew member's name Hunter?" Tomahawk asked with a big smile of triumph.

"How did you know?"

"Because Hunter was the doctor's son, and the man I worked for, they're one in the same person."

Miles was shocked.

"Hunter was there when you killed his old man and decided to set the fire to burn the place down for the insurance. He's not even a real sailor type. He took that job because he wanted to be with you to set his plan B in motion."

"Plan B?" Miles asked.

"Yeah, after you went into the wind Stella started having second thoughts about you, feeling bad that she had screwed you. She was also hitting up Hunter for chunks of money, to help buy all kinds of toys and shit for the baby when it arrived. If Hunter objected, she threatened to tell the police. You know, she was becoming a pain in the ass; in his words, not mine. So, Hunter decided to get rid of her too, but he needed someone to not only do the dirty work but take the fall. He told you the truth on the ship because he knew you were…"

"…an aggressive man who would kill her", Miles finished the sentence.

"Hunter set you up from the jump. He followed you from the boat and called the police the minute you arrived at your wife's place. So, now he's living large and here you are," Tomahawk ended his story.

"It was him… the man I saw outside my house that day," Miles added.

"Sorry, man, I had to tell you all about it. I knew you were in this prison, but I wondered if I was ever going to meet you and here we are together."

"You know what?" Miles asked.

"Tell me…" Tomahawk said.

"I'm not going to die in here. I have a hole in my gut that's burning for revenge. Me and you are going to figure out a way out of this place. I'm going to get back to Darkness Falls and kill that bastard." Miles swore an oath to himself.

Tomahawk said, "I'm in."

Miles laid in the dark that night, planning.

SHARP

R. J. ERBACHER

I came to Darkness Falls a while ago because of my man, Dolan. An acquaintance got him a job here that was going to pay him big. We planned to stay for six months. I was going to get a waitress job and we'd make do in some tiny apartment and bank his whole check, live off mine and in half a years' time we would have enough money to start off on the right foot down in Alabama or Mississippi were the living was cheap and the sun always shines and the weather was warm. And damn do I look good in a bikini. Everything was all set. Except Darkness Falls didn't cooperate. This town turned my existence into a dumpster of sordid waste.

The minute we pulled into this place, nearly flipping the car on a sharp curve into town, I felt the change. It was just turning dark when we arrived and it was like somebody pulled a curtain down over us. Not one of those frilly things you see hung on the windows of nice homes but a black out curtain that blocks out all the light from outside. First off, the apartment was worse than we expected, dreadful and dirty, with loud neighbors and bad plumbing. Sometimes the water worked, most of the time, not so much. And the manager was a low life, looking me up and down and licking his lips every time I walked through the lobby. Yeah, I found a job fairly quick in a bar, place called

'The Watering Hole' that served food and drinks but the pay was crap and the tips were awful. And on top of that, because I was good-looking all the customers assumed I was a whore and tried propositioning me every night. That pissed Dolan off big time and he kept telling me to quit or find another place to work. But work around here was not easy to come by, especially one within walking distance. I heard there was another bar, Vicky's, that paid better but they were way on the other side of town and I couldn't schlep all the way there. You see, we had to sell Dolan's car to get some starting capital and he used mine to get back and forth to work so I got to trudge through the rain and the gloom to get to the bar and then the dark, dark night coming home which believe me, was pretty damn scary.

His job as production foreman was not all it was supposed to be either. The money was good but the conditions of the factory were terrible. The lighting was bad and the place stunk like sewer. He said they had rodents in there that were as big as raccoons. You would spot them skulking around in the dark corners, never really getting a good look at them but you could sense that they were huge. Dolan said he wasn't even sure that they were real rats but he couldn't say what they might be. His workers freaked him out as well just by their appearance. He couldn't look anybody in the eye, their faces were all a little off, disturbing sneers and such. On top of everything he had an obese, terrible boss who would watch from his office that overlooked the factory and he kept accusing him of slacking off and stealing tools, two things I later found out were both true.

We figured we'd tough it out and make the best of a bad situation but things went from bad to worse. There were fights every other night in the bar and I nearly got my head taken off a few times by thrown bottles or flying chairs. Arnie, the boss there, a heavy-set bearded guy, wanted to pull in business and told me I had to wear low cut shirts and short skirts, which didn't help my reputation none. Many times, I had to fend off guys who got too touchy-feely. The stainless-steel tray I carried to transport drinks and plates of food became both a Viking shield and a weapon. It had a flattened curve on one side where somebody must have dropped something heavy on it and that edge was sharp enough that I could probably take some guy's limb off with it, or some other proffered appendage, with a quick chop. Most of the time it was enough to just use it as a buffer between me and them, although once I had to use it like a cartoon frying pan to bonk some guy on the head to settle him down.

There was also this one creepy customer who kept coming into The Watering Hole just to stare at me. Long black coat and fedora, always with his face in shadows. The first time he came in I went over to his booth, he didn't order anything, didn't even pick up his head. I said to him he had to order something or he would have to leave. Five minutes later Arnie told me to take the guy's drink to his table. I had no idea how he ordered it but I brought it and stayed away from him for the rest of the night. He started coming in two, three times a week. Every time he showed up, he'd do the same thing, not talking, just staring, and it spooked me something terrible. One time when Dolan was there drinking and the guy came in, I told him to go over and speak to him, threaten him that he'd better leave me alone. Dolan took one look at the guy and refused, saying that there was a bad vibe coming from him.

Dolan wasn't having any better luck with his career. Three months after he started, the place closed up. He tried finding another job but none of them paid as well as the one he came here for. He ended up doing part time interior demolition which was a significant pay cut meaning we'd have to stay longer than anticipated. The pressure was so rough he started drinking heavily and spending a lot of money on it as well. He kept dipping into our little 'nest egg' to pay for his alcohol. We were storing all of our hard-earned cash that we saved in a peanut can in the closet and he would go in there to skim, thinking I didn't know. The worst nights were when he came to my place while I was working and because Arnie liked him, he gave him every other drink for free, thinking it would make me happy. But then he would get hammered and try brawling with any customer that even hinted at hitting on me and the night would always end bad. Sure, everybody else he could harass but the creeper guy he was afraid of. The two of us started fighting with each other at the apartment too and we wound up becoming the louder neighbors. I sported a black eye or three into work over the next month but Dolan got a knee in the balls in retaliation for one of them and I guess he still has the nail grooves on his cheeks from where I fended him off on a particularly nasty Friday night.

I also started noticing that it kept getting darker and darker, even in the daytime and although it never was really sunny, always cloudy or misty, the days seemed to be turning into perpetual dusk. The bar never had great lighting, I think Arnie kept it that way so people won't see what a shithole it was, but when I went to the window each morning to see what the weather was like, I found myself bug-eyed in search of sunshine. It got to the point that when I took orders on my pad, I had to squint to see what I had just written on the paper. I figured it was my eyesight and I thought about going to an optometrist. But when Dolan said he thought the lamps in the apartment were getting duller I knew it wasn't just me. Right from when I was hired there were lots of stories babbling around the bar about people losing their eyesight. Some slowly and temporarily and others instantly going blind while driving and crashing into poles or other people. I figured they were just bullshit, tall tales, urban legends, but when I began to realize it was happening to me, I started getting a bad feeling about Darkness Falls. That maybe there was something really wrong to this place. One night when I was off and Dolan wasn't drunk and we weren't hostile with each other, a rarity for all three to happen at once, I suggested that since things weren't working out, we should get the hell out of this town. He looked at me like I was crazy, almost as if he really wanted to stay, that he liked being in Darkness Falls. Shit, was I ever wrong.

I came home from work a week or so later around four AM, was drenched from walking home in the rain and totally exhausted. I'd had a real hard night with all the crazies in the bar. The cherry on my night was when my creeper with the hat and coat came in and towards the end of my shift he painfully grabbed my wrist as I walked by. He took the tray away and turned my hand up to an open palm. I thought he might want me to do something kinky but he placed a shiny metal object gently there. I had no clue what it was, it resembled something like a barbed hook that went on the end of a chain whip used by the demons in hell. He then said the only word he ever said to me.

"Sharp."

And it looked it. If I had closed my hand into a fist, I felt like my fingers would be severed off. If this was a gift from my shadowy stalker, it was a crappy gift. I had no idea what it was or what to do with it. I nodded my thanks and brought it behind the bar for safe keeping. A feeling came over me that now that he had given me something I owed him something in return. When I left work that rainy night, I kept looking over my shoulder the whole way home thinking he was right behind me. Or maybe hiding in an alley in front of me. I was so rattled when I got to the apartment that I double locked the door, stripped off my wet clothes, left them in a puddle on the floor and crawled into bed. Dolan wasn't home, I didn't know where he was nor did I care.

The next day, I woke around noon and went to take a shower but of course there was no running water. I settled for a cup of coffee but when I got to the kitchen the coffee machine was missing. Man, was I pissed. I figured the son of a bitch had probably hocked it for drinking money. But when I went to the fridge, I saw that the beer wasn't there either. Now I was worried. I ran through the living room; the TV was gone. So was his laptop, all his clothes from the bedroom and the keys to my car. I made a mad dash for the metal can of nuts in the cabinet, hoping against hope, but he had emptied it. Dolan had taken everything and split, leaving me exactly twenty-three bucks from last night's tips to my name. He even had the gall to take my few pieces of jewelry, the only thing I still had from my mother. I had brought that chunk of metal oddity home last night from the stranger and I smacked it off the table in frustration and ripped a gash in my palm. There was a quarter bottle of vodka left, he'd taken all his scotch, and I sat in the dry tub alternating between disinfecting my cut and drinking my breakfast. I was broke and alone in Darkness Falls.

And yet, I hadn't hit rock bottom. The apartment manager came to me two days later claiming the rent was overdue, Dolan never paid him. I explained my situation to him and he was deviously sympathetic. The only way he would give me an extra week to pay up was if I agreed to an 'oral' arrangement with him. I was also forced into sneaking food from work, stooping to taking half eaten sandwiches off plates when I cleared the tables and scarfing them down before I had a chance to actually consider how low I had sunk. All the time my eyesight continued to diminish. I could see clearly, it just seemed that I was trying to function in somebody's unfinished basement that was lit by a single bulb. My goal had now been reduced to saving enough money to buy a bus ticket out of this pit of despair. Hopefully before my sight went completely dark. I figured I had three weeks if I really scrimped.

While lying in bed each night all I could think about was how drastically my life had turned the minute I stepped foot into Darkness Falls. Everything was supposed to work out. We had a plan, a good one, and it all should have gone smoothly but you know what they say about plans. You make plans and God laughs. Somehow, I didn't think it was God. Somebody was laughing all right, but I don't even think God visited Darkness Falls. Whether it was Fate or Karma or Destiny, they were having a grand old time messing with my life. Not long after, it all went to hell.

I was one paycheck away from having enough to pull up stakes and try again. Anywhere else. It was almost closing on a Wednesday night and the bar was near empty. The last few customers left and the cook had finished his chores and was gone, leaving just me and Arnie, the last one's cleaning down the counters and fixing the stools. I was carrying my tray with a few dirty dishes on it and wiping the last table when he took a call on his cell phone and started mumbling excitedly. Then he hung up, grabbed his jacket and tossed me the keys telling me to lock up, he had a family emergency to take care of, leaving in a rush. I'd never closed before, not by myself, or been alone in the bar. I had to stop a minute and think what I should do. There was no one around so I could do whatever I wanted. I thought about going into the kitchen and pilfering me a real dinner which I hadn't had since Dolan left. I was on a steady diet of garbage scraps, no-brand cereal and PB and J. There were no cameras in the place, Arnie would never spring for that expense. I could eat whatever I wanted from the kitchen fridge. I headed that way anticipating a four-course meal when I walked past the register and jerked to a halt. Arnie had left in such a hurry that he hadn't pulled the money from the draw. I'd worked the register all the time. I knew how to open it. Was this my opportunity? I had never stolen anything in my life except maybe a pack of gum from the convenience store once or twice as a teenager. But now I would be a full-fledged criminal. Obviously, Arnie would know it was me who took the till and no matter where I went, I would have a record, my face on a wanted poster. Did they still do that? What if I took just enough to get that bus ticket? Arnie never kept track; he might not even miss it. Didn't I deserve a break? Wasn't I the person who got shafted in this deal? I worked for my money, I was just taking an early withdrawal of what was mine, right? Well?

As I was contemplating all this, I unknowingly moved closer to the register. I put the tray on the counter. My hands were on the buttons. I was ringing up a 'no sale.' The draw was springing open. The cash was there. All I had to do was grab it. I had to really look hard with my fading vision to see what was in the bill slots. How much should I take?

Then a noise made me spin around and I realized I wasn't alone. A figure was slowly approaching. I could barely make him out as he crept towards me but I recognized the outline of the long coat and hat. How had we missed him when we were closing up? Maybe he was in the bathroom? I had to renegotiate where I was in reference to the front door. Could I get there before him? Not likely. Not with my bad eyesight. Which actually seemed to be worsening with each deliberate step closer he took. Was he the reason I was slipping into darkness? All this had started right around the time he showed up at the bar. Could he control the dark? I snatched up my tray and tossed the contents at him, the plates crashed onto the floor in pieces. The assault had not daunted him in the slightest. I pulled the server's shield to my chest in defense, maybe I could block an attack. I was trapped by the darkness and the creeper who were both enveloping me. Was this my penalty for contemplating the robbery? No bad deed goes unpunished or something like that. This was the culmination of my sentence in Darkness Falls.

In a last gasp effort, I flung the tray at him. I heard a thwack, the tray must have hit him, and then it clanged onto the floor like metallic thunder, thumping along with something else. I could barely make out his form, standing just a few steps away but not coming forward. Was he toying with me? Drawing out the suspense to make me suffer. Could I have made him angrier? A few seconds passed with nothing happening and I was on the verge of screaming because I didn't know what else to do when he just toppled backwards landing in a resounding thud amongst the shattered pieces of the plates. That's when my sight left me totally. My world was now utterly black, in more ways than one.

I was lost in a dark chasm of confusion. A man I had seriously hurt was lying at my feet. The door to escape was a dash away. A register full of money to steal was nearby. And I could see none of them. I was filled with contradiction and contrition. What had I done? How could I undo it? There was no way. I felt an overwhelming pressure on my soul and shoulders. The man at my feet had never done a single thing to me. He might have been creepy but that wasn't a crime. If it were, half the population of Darkness Falls would be locked up. I had to see if the guy was all right. I went down to my hands and knees and felt around until I touched his shoe. I shook it but there was no response. I inched closer, my hand shaking each part of his body in the hopes he would rouse. I got up to his chest and felt around for a heart beat but with his coat on I couldn't feel anything. The best way would be to put my fingers on the side of his neck like they do in all those medical shows. I crawled my hands up his chest past his collar. I reached up to his neck to find a pulse. There wasn't one. Not a pulse. There wasn't a neck. Or head.

My fingers fell into the wet sticky cavity of his hollow throat that was still expanding and contracting, gasping to take in one last breath. Blood spurted into my grasp. I couldn't see my hands but I felt the viscera sticking to them as I pulled them away. I fell back onto my ass and put my arms out for support and my palm planted onto the nose and open eyes of his head, my fingertips brushing the fedora, still firmly in place. Now I screamed as if it was my intention to deafen every person in Darkness Falls. I had lost my sight, I wanted them to lose their hearing. I brought my hands up to my face and felt the soggy gore on my cheeks and screamed louder. I expected my neck to explode like his neck had. The sharp end of the tray must have caught him at the right spot when I frisbeed it and sliced through his throat and separated his vertebrae. Took the head clean off. What were the chances? Only me. When I could no longer gather a breath to shriek, I sat there trembling, trying to decide what to do.

'Help yourself. Get up,' my mind ordered me. So, I did. I reached around until my hand grabbed the edge of the register and used it for support. When I got to wobbly feet my hands came away with bills stuck to the drying blood. I tried to shake them free but they wouldn't come loose. I scraped them against my shirt and skirt until they were off. What was I going to do? How do I explain this to Arnie? To the police? No one was going to believe that I killed him by accident. My bloody hand prints were all over him. Or that I wasn't trying to steal the money. Not really. My blood was on that as well. That I had suddenly gone blind. Please. At that instant I could no longer stand being in that bar with the body and the blood and the money. I sightlessly weaved in the direction of the door and came close and soon found the handle. Outside I wondered if there was anybody around who would see a blood drenched woman flailing around at four in the morning on an empty sidewalk. I had to be careful to not go into the road and get run down. I staggered for an undetermined distance using the sides of buildings for support. A few minutes later I reached an alleyway that I had remembered seeing in my travels. It seemed like the only place I could reasonably go right now to get off the streets and at least try and think what to do next. I fell over a garbage can, tore my shirt on a wire fence, scared a stray cat away and finally came to a brick wall at the dead end of the alley. I was feeling around for a comfortable place to collapse when I heard a gruff male voice.

"You can't be here."

"What?" I said, turning in that general direction.

"What the hell happened to you!"

"I...I..." was all that came out.

"You kill somebody?"

"No! I...I...It was...?" I started to cry.

"Sit down before you fall down."

The guy with the gruff voice guided me to what was a collection of smashed up boxes and crumpled up newspapers and sat me into a heap then delicately touched my cheek, stroked my hair.

"Rest a minute."

"I…I can't see," I blurted out.

"No kidding. You hungry?"

"Yes," I whimpered.

"Well, you've got a bloody ten-dollar bill stuck to your skirt. I'm just going to take that and get us a couple cups of coffee and some donuts. After breakfast we'll get you cleaned up and settled. Then we'll talk about our living arrangements. Don't worry, everything's going to work out. I hope you don't snore."

That's how I became the blind homeless woman of this town. And now because I depend on yet another man for everything, I am condemned to stay in Darkness Falls. Forever.

SHADOW ORDER

BRADLEY H. SINOR

Rayne

The penthouse worried me, more because of what wasn't there than what was.

Under other circumstances I would have loved to kick back, drop my shoes on the floor, grab a bottle of wine and just stare out at the night. This place didn't really have much of a view. So many penthouses that I'd been in before did; LA, New York, London. Not Darkness Falls. But these weren't ordinary circumstances and that wasn't what I was interested in doing this evening.

Of course, Christopher James Alexander IV had his own expectations of what *I* was going to be doing this evening, specifically, screwing his brains out. Christopher was not really my type. I like men with a little more humanity than he had. But he was the assignment for tonight and I wasn't about to let him think things weren't going his way, even though they weren't.

I caught a glimpse of the two of us in a mirror on the wall. He topped out at six foot one, and believe me, the muscles under that jacket were real. I have to admit that I looked pretty damn good, myself. My whole outfit, from the red mini-dress with the spaghetti straps and the dangerously low cleavage-revealing neckline along with expensive shoes and silver blonde hair, had been designed to appeal to him.

I could just imagine the housekeeping staff moving in when Christopher left for the evening to get it ready to impress whoever "the boss" might bring home, be it for business or pleasure. In the process of doing that, they removed all traces that a real person actually lived here.

The problem was the Magick, specifically, the security wards I could sense that lay over the penthouse, in fact, over the whole building. They weren't all that special, almost off-the-shelf type of security spells, the kind anybody can buy. I had better Magickal security on my rent-controlled two-bedroom apartment than there seemed to be here.

It was like they were asking to get robbed.

So I did the only logical thing to do right then. I fluttered my eyelashes at Chris-boy and gave him my best come-fuck-me smile. Of course, he didn't have the slightest idea of what I had in mind for *him*.

"Do you live alone, or do we have to worry about your parents coming home?" I giggled as I slid onto the couch next to him, feeling his arms wrap around me. Let's just say this guy was definitely living up to his reputation as a womanizer. But at least he knew how to kiss, and to do it very well. I may have been there on business, but there was nothing that said I couldn't enjoy myself.

I had spent three weeks watching this guy, not to mention letting him see me, at the right locations and with the right people.

"You owe me a drink, mister," I said rather breathlessly, when we finally came up for air.

"Ms. Salvatore, your wish is my command," he said.

"I told you to call me Zoë."

He grinned as he expertly filled two tall thin champagne flutes, then spooned some patte onto a cracker and passed it over to me.

As far as Christopher or any of the people who moved in his social circle knew, my name was Zoë Salvatore, pronounced, I had emphatically told them, without the e on the end.

There was a rumor that my father or my uncle or some close male relative was a high- ranking member of the Unione Corse, the Corsican

Mafia of France. There were big plans for Darkness Falls. This was going to become the home operations of the US faction of the organization. It was a tale that had been rather expertly whispered into just the right ears, which then got told to someone else, who happened to mention it, just in passing of course, to other people, and as a result, it came to the attention of the people that I wanted to hear it. None of those people knew, and if I had my way, would never know, that the name on my legitimate driver's license was Rayne Traven.

As I leaned over to nibble on Christopher's ear, I dropped a small pill that I had carried inside my bracelet, into his drink. In only a matter of a second or two it dissolved.

I was relaxing back against the leather sofa, letting my head rest on his shoulder, when Christopher said something that just didn't fit the ambience.

"So, my sweet Zoë, are you going to tell me what you are really here for now, or would you prefer to wait until we have fucked our brains out? I mean, after all, you're good, very good, but I saw you putting something into my glass."

"What are you talking about?"

That was when he grabbed my shoulders and literally lifted me up off the couch, turning me over in the air and slamming me hard onto the top of the marble coffee table. In the process, my glass was knocked over and the food tray flew out onto the floor, making one hell of a stain on the white carpet that stretched over half the room.

"I don't know what you're talking about," I gasped, the sharp pain in the back of my head and along my back running through me like a linebacker. My dress got shoved up and my black G-string was exposed "Look, if you're into something really kinky, I can handle that. Everybody's got a few kinks; I can show you some of mine if you show me yours."

He slapped me, twice.

Christopher had one hand on my shoulder holding me down. I reached up to try and push him away with my left hand; he grabbed it and pushed it down over my head. That brought him close enough so that his face was within a few inches of mine.

I pushed my right hand up and hit him on the neck, driving my highly polished fingernails as deep into his flesh as I could. Then I dragged them down, leaving lines of blood in the wake. Talk about your DNA evidence. It felt like I had a pound of skin under my nails. So much for my expensive manicure.

He screamed, jerked back and was about to get really, really nasty with me when he just stopped in mid-movement, eyes gone glassy, and looked at me like he didn't know where he was or what was going on.

Then he fell forward, right on top of me. Now, I weigh a hundred and five pounds soaking wet. Christopher James Alexander IV, on the other hand, weighed around twice that much and was at least six inches taller than me.

"That's going to leave a couple of bruises," I sputtered.

For the next minute or two I didn't do anything, just tried to breathe, which was definitely not easy. All Christopher did was start snoring, a very nasal and disgusting sound, and having it in my face was just outrightly gross! If I hadn't been hurting so much, I probably would have laughed.

When I tried to push him off, I had no success. Moving over two hundred pounds of dead weight while lying flat on your back isn't easy! Finally, after my third attempt, recalling those urban legends of someone pinned in a bathtub under a body and the only way they got free was to go cannibal, I decided it was time to get really serious.

I was just about to try a levitation spell when I heard a funny sound under my head. It was kind of a metal sound, crossed with an egg cracking. Then all of a sudden the world shifted and I felt myself dumped to the right. The elegant table was not designed for the combined weight and buckled. The movement sent Christopher rolling that way as well, so he ended up half on me and half laying on the floor.

I was just glad it broke. I hadn't been all that confident in a levitation spell that I hadn't practiced in a long time. This way I had leverage enough to just push my companion off of me, into a heap between the splintered coffee table and the couch.

Once I was on my feet, which were none too steady for the moment, and rearranged my clothes, I headed straight over to the bar, ignoring him completely. I wanted to kick the SOB but I had other plans for him shortly. I had noticed a squat green and tan bottle there earlier. I focused on it and read the words Tullamore Dew on the front. I am not much of a drinker, but right then I needed something strong that would deaden some of the pain, and it actually tasted pretty damn good.

I looked at the middle fingernail on my right hand and couldn't help but smile. I could still see some of the glitter that I had so carefully applied earlier. You could hardly tell it from the stuff I used on my other nails; it looked spectacular, if I do say so myself. I figure if everything else went down the toilet I could always get a job in a nail salon. The fact that mixed in with that polish was a special solution of a contact knock-out drug certainly came in handy. The only problem with the drug is that it normally takes three to five minutes to take effect. I had fixed that with a tiny bit of Magick to speed up the chemical reaction. Unfortunately, the one ingredient I needed to make it work quickly was adrenaline; mine, massive dose of it. That's why I let him see me drug his drink.

Normally I prefer getting my adrenaline rushes in other ways, a lot less painful ways, but you have to use what resources are available.

I ran my fingers along Christopher's cheek chanting a few ancient words. After several seconds he drowsily opened his eyes. They were unfocused and it was hard to tell if there was any awareness behind them. He drew a couple of breaths and mumbled something and then dropped off. I think what he said was something like "duck painting." I considered trying to prod him for more, but at that point I wasn't sure I would get anything else, or if I did, it would make any more sense than what he had said.

Jacob Duck was a well-known baroque artist from the 1630s. I heard his originals went for quite a bit, when you could get someone to turn loose of them. So that's what I looked for.

The duck painting turned out not to be Jacob, but rather, Daffy. On one wall was a rather large black velvet painting of Daffy Duck, his hand extended up into the air, and I would have liked to suspect that he was loudly proclaiming that it was "Wabbit season!"

The safe wasn't behind the painting, but rather just to the side;

Daffy wasn't just pointing at an off-stage Bugs, but at the safe itself. Once I had the panel open and could see the safe, I felt like I had run up against a brick wall. The safe was a solid steel M-5 Vorillia design complete with about a half dozen different locking mechanisms built in. Not that I couldn't get through those; they would just take time.

The other stuff was what frustrated me. Besides the physical locks there were protective wards out the ying-yang. Just standing close to them for more than a couple of minutes made me feel antsy, like there were bugs crawling all over my arms. *This* was the high-class alarm system I had been expecting since Christopher and I had climbed out of his car.

I understood now that this whole thing was a set up to nail any intruders, lull them into a false sense of security with the off-the-shelf protections, and then stomp down hard when the prize was within reach.

"Okay, I can play, too," I said to the sleeping jerk on the floor.

Disarming the Magick alarms around the rest of the apartment wasn't that much of a problem. I had it done in less than five minutes. Now it was time to call in some assistance. I went out onto the balcony, the chilly air making me shiver, looking out over the cityscape, and took a second to be repulsed by the scenery. Pus-yellow clouds dissipated through the black sky dusting all the gray concrete slabs that were scattered below it. But at least it was above all the crappy structures at street level. How this shit managed to land the best pieces of real estate in Darkness Falls was a mystery? He probably had some good connections too.

I took a minute to gaze into the infinite blackness and decided to get back to work. Taking a green laser pointer from my purse, I pointed it out over the railing at a building just across the way and a few stories taller. Even that short distance the beam had a hard time cutting through the murk. Three blinks with it were answered a few seconds later by three blinks with a red pointer that hit the wall just behind me; it then did a wide circle on the wall and vanished.

That little signal translated into "Move your ass out of the way."

Maybe thirty seconds after that a three-foot long harpoon buried itself into brick and mortar; a long metal cable strung out loosely behind it and smashed into the wall next to the patio door. The harpoon had not even stopped vibrating before the cable rose up until it was a tight line vanishing off into the emptiness, angled upwards.

It wasn't until he was more than half way across that I could make out the silhouette of a figure sliding along the line, arms pulled in against the chest and legs clenched tightly to make everything as aerodynamic as possible. Less than a minute later the figure landed on the patio and stumbled to a stop just in front of the wall.

"Hi, Sis," said the new arrival. "I heard that there was a good party here; thought I would crash it."

"Took you long enough, little brother," I said.

Noah

At first glance, watching a beautiful woman prancing around wearing a whole lot of very little might seem like a fun way to pass the evening. But not when she's your sister!

It is even more not fun when she is in a nice warm penthouse apartment, but you are stuck on the roof of a sixteen-story building looking down on her through a set of high powered military grade night vision binoculars. The strain on the eyes trying to keep focus in this gritty haze was giving me a headache. And trust me, any time of year, roofs are no picnic. They can be cold and windy and miserable and I'd been on my fair share of them. This one was all three.

Unfortunately, I didn't have a whole lot of choice in the matter. The firm of R&N Consulting, Ltd, which is my sister and myself, had bank accounts that appreciated occasional replenishment.

Just as soon as the laser pointer signaled on the wall behind me, I began to move. I sighted in on Rayne, who was standing with her hands on her hips staring up in my general direction and looking not real happy with me.

The clamps absorbed a lot of the recoil, but it still kicked like a son-of-a-bitch when I pulled the trigger, in spite of my Dragonskin armor. I knew that when I looked, I would have a bruise on my shoulder, but that I could live with. But it worked, hitting within an inch of where I was aiming. Three minutes later there was a tight zip line running from the sixteenth floor of the Hammett building to the thirteenth floor (Fourteenth technically since there was no floor thirteen) penthouse of the Alexander building.

I may be an adrenaline junkie, like my sister, and willing to risk my life doing things, but I like to be able to walk away from them, and if I fell from this height, that sure wouldn't be my idea of fun.

Rayne came over to me, a look of concern on her face; as to whether it was sisterly concern or concern about being able to finish this job, I didn't ask, and she wouldn't have told me if her life depended on it.

"Hi, sis," I said. "I heard that there was a good party here; thought I would crash it."

"Took you long enough, little brother."

I pulled myself up, eyeing her in silence. Actually, her little jibe made me comfortable. I would have been worried if my darling sister had not said something rude to me, in which case I would figure she was probably either really mad at me, or sick.

"Sis, before we get started, I do have one question?" I asked as I unclipped the harness from the pulley reel.

"What?" she snapped.

"Aren't you cold?"

Rayne cocked her head at me then looked down at herself, then smiled. "Of course it's cold, but sometimes fashion is worth putting up with minor discomforts."

"You're kind of old to pull that look off, you know."

"Shut the hell up and get to work."

I could see Christopher lying in a heap between a semi-demolished coffee table and the sofa.

"Looks to me like you were getting a bit rough there. Developing some new interests which you would care to share with your brother?" I had long ago learned what buttons I could push with Rayne.

I knew things had taken a really weird turn as I entered the room and saw the black velvet painting of Daffy Duck. I made a mental note to get one for myself.

"I say we go to red alert and film the rest of the episode on the battle bridge," I told Rayne. She replied with standard issue glare number 832, which translates as "shut up, stupid brother, and let's get serious."

The actual physical lock mechanism was a keypad with a hand scanner right next to it. I'd bet dollars to doughnuts that the scanner could tell if the hand was still alive or had been chopped off of its owner for convenience.

"I can bypass the first of the wards," I told Rayne. "But then we're going to need your boyfriend over here when it comes to the actual lock."

"He's not my boyfriend." She snapped.

So while she went to rouse sleeping beauty with a kiss, I turned my attention back to the safe. Taking a deep breath, I held it for a ten count then slowly let it out.

Magick is many things, call it what you may and disguise it with any kind of fancy frou-frou ceremonies, but when it comes right down to it, its energy arranged and rearranged in a particular order by people who can tap into it. Had he lived long enough, I suspect, ol' Albert Einstein might have discovered Magick, and become very good with it.

I won't say it was easy, but I basically let the first couple of layers of wards reflect back into themselves, sort of thinking that they were still working, but they weren't.

I felt Rayne's presence, her thoughts intertwining with mine as we did the same thing, plus a few variations on it, to the other wards. The trick to the whole thing is that most people who ward something do it with the idea of one person trying to break in and keeping them out. Having two people trying to bypass the same set of protections at the same time makes things a whole lot easier.

I stepped away from the safe as the last of the magical alarms slipped into neutral, my throat as dry as Death Valley at noon. Rayne was standing next to me, one hand on my shoulder, the other wrapped around lover boy.

Rayne

Never, ever, think that the plan that seems so perfect when you have been staring at maps and diagrams for hours, trying to brainstorm out every possible contingency, is going to work just exactly the way you want it to.

While Noah was doing his thing with the safe, I tried to wake up Christopher, only to realize just how much of a fluke it must have been that I had been able to get anything out of him earlier. I didn't think that the drug I had knocked Christopher out with was going to be so effective.

No matter what I did, from shaking him to forcing him to sit up to yelling at him seemed enough to rouse him. Even a slap in the face, which was gratifying, didn't help.

"Tell him you want to do him against the wall," Noah chimed in. I ignored my brother's suggestion without comment, especially since I had already tried that and had not gotten a reaction, a fact that didn't help my ego.

I was about ready to have Noah help me drag him over to the safe; let's see him stay asleep doing that! Then it occurred to me to try one more thing.

I leaned up next to his ear and said "Chris, Chris! You've got to hurry! It's time for school."

Don't ask me why, but that seemed to do it. "Wha….Wha…..the iguana ate my homework. Can I take the flying monkeys to school with me for show and tell?"

Iguanas? Flying monkeys? Christopher must have had some really strange pets when he was growing up.

That done, I maneuvered Chris over next to Noah whose eyes were closed and his forehead was covered with a sheen of perspiration. I know that everybody who does Magick sees the results differently when they immerse themselves in the flow of energy.

There was a slight buzzing in my ears, but that passed quickly.

I seemed to have found the key to getting Christopher moving. I just told him it was time to get dressed for school, which got him on his feet. I half carried - half guided him drunkenly to the wall.

Without any prompting, and keeping his hand on the scanner, Christopher leaned over and put his right eye up to the tube. I heard something, but I wasn't sure what, then the tube pulled back into the keypad and the light on the hand scanner turned from green to white. I released him and Christopher grinned and thumped down onto his ass, humming something that sounded like "TipToe through the Tulips," and then he fainted into a prone position, stretched out on the floor and began to snore, again.

The door to the safe popped open just like a microwave door.

"What about the keypad?" asked Noah. "Retinal and palm identification makes sense, but isn't there a code that should go into the keypad?"

"Maybe we're overthinking this; the keypad might just be a decoy that sets off another alarm."

There was one way to find out; I pulled the safe door completely open.

Nothing happened.

Inside were some expensive jewelry, a whole shitpot full of cash, which I was willing to wager was completely untraceable, and what we had come for, a silver metal briefcase.

The possibility that there might be some sort of balance alarm occurred to me, but I figured we might as well risk it. I could sense no Magick about the thing, but that didn't mean that there wasn't any, just that if there was, it had been concealed well. I still wasn't sure.

I reminded myself about overthinking.

Noah

Before Sis wasted the whole night contemplating whether or not there were any booby traps I reached into the safe and grabbed the briefcase. I waited, counting off ten seconds, and nothing happened, no sirens, no alarms, nothing, which was exactly what I wanted to hear.

"We don't even talk about luck until we are out of here and having drinks somewhere," she said.

"Come on Sis. Have a little faith in me for once."

I checked the case, saw it was locked, not Magik locked, just regular old steel hasps; we could worry about that later when we had time back in our office. I handed it to her and began to prowl around the apartment, perusing in and out among the curtains and what I suspected were moveable panels that could give a visitor to the penthouse the feeling of being in a maze if they were arranged correctly. I wanted to make sure nobody was coming out of the woodwork to sneak up on us. To be honest, I should have done this first but not everything goes by the book. I stopped at the bar for a double shot of Tullamore Dew to wet my whistle and bolster my confidence as I took one last turn through the room.

Satisfied that all was kosher I turned to Rayne and looked her over.

"Time for the real show to begin," and I unzipped my black jumpsuit.

It took a little longer than expected. I was a bit fatigued from the exertion so far tonight but I think I pulled it off with some flare.

Christopher James Alexander IV said, "My dear Zoë, I must say you have made this evening, shall we say, quite a unique experience for me."

Rayne

A few minutes later I heard a sound behind me and was almost startled when I heard, "My dear Zoë…"

I stared at the doppelgänger that was Christopher James Alexander IV for a few minutes; studying him from the tips of his highly polished shoes right up to the part in his hair.

'Yes, I think you'll do,' I thought, which was exactly the same thing I had said to the real Christopher earlier this evening. He had actually taken my words as a challenge, the gorgeous woman with the mysterious slightly sinister family connections. It would have taken a lot to make him walk away.

Noah finished with, "you have made this evening, shall we say, quite a unique experience for me,"

"I hope to God that you aren't anywhere close to believing that line of bull, brother. I also hope that your usual pickup lines are a lot better than that, otherwise the only thing you are going to be doing is sleeping alone most of the time."

"Now that is hitting below the belt," he said. "Besides, would it hurt you to say something complimentary, elderly sister of mine?"

"I give compliments when they're deserved. Your ego is big enough as it is; there is no need for me to pump it any higher, little brother." I looked him up and down. "I'm amazed that one of his tuxes fit you. I'd say he has you by about twenty pounds and a good two inches."

Noah chuckled. "Hey, the power of some safety pins and a couple of pieces of strategically placed double stick tape."

I'll give Noah points. Most people I've run across who can do 'glamours' do every visible inch, clothes and face. Noah preferred to just do faces and hands, adding in real clothes rather than illusions, fewer things that could go wrong. He was a dead ringer for my date tonight.

"Like I said, I think you'll do, at least in terms of getting us past the security guards. I really don't fancy having to run in these shoes," I said.

"Those guards will be spending their time looking at you, my dear," he said. "Otherwise, there is something drastically wrong with them."

I checked sleepy-time Christopher once more; it took a moment to be sure he was still breathing. I resisted the temptation to put his socks on his hands, a pair of panties over his face and scribble "I had a wonderful time" in lipstick on his chest; but since the panties would have to be mine and I didn't bring any extra, I decided to forget that idea.

"I'm in the mood for being somewhere else where something exciting is happening," said Noah.

"As far as anyone who sees us is concerned, there's been a lot of action tonight and you've been on the receiving end of it," I said.

"True." He straightened his bowtie with a grin and extended his arm to me. "So what do you say we get the hell out of here?"

"I like the way you think, little brother."

"After you, older sister."

Noah

Walking out the front door made a lot more sense to me than rappelling down the side of a building, which we had been forced to do on more than one occasion in the past. Besides there were guards at ground level that would have to be fought off.

In this business, simple is the way to go.

I had found some hair samples in Chrissy's bathroom on his brush, dyed, I noticed. It took just a little bit of Magick to tap the DNA and Christopher James Alexander IV was looking back from his bathroom mirror at me. Egotist, ladies' man, and all-around shit.

Besides, all we had to do was fool a few security guards who weren't smart enough to keep from getting assigned to the graveyard shift. If the guards weren't complete eunuchs, they would be watching Rayne, rather than me or the metal case dangling loosely in my hand. Christopher often carried this case we knew from the surveillance photos but late at night, not so much.

As we walked from the apartment Rayne laid her head on my shoulder and softly whispered. "Do you think he would have been paranoid enough to rig the elevator so the guards could watch what was going on?"

"Maybe he figured to get some shots of himself and the current date getting hot and heavy even before they hit the penthouse. So we need to keep character," I answered.

"Why, of course, darling! You were simply wonderful, and I do have some stupendous plans for you later," she said.

"That's fantastic."

I grinned as I reached down and grabbed Rayne's ass and gave it a good hard squeeze. She had a sudden intake of breath and let out a distinct moan of enjoyment. I figured if there was anyone watching, this was exactly what they would expect to see. That was all they were going to get to see; I drew the line at some things, like kissing my sister, even in the line of duty.

"Watch it buster," she said. "Remember my trusted agents know exactly where you sleep."

She was referring to her two cats, the gray terrors, Gandalf and

Morgaine, who seem to be able to slip through solid walls and get past locked doors. Those two beasts also took great delight in tormenting me when I came by her place for a visit. and they had nasty claws.

"Remind me to lock them in the basement and lose the key," I muttered.

"Yeah, right, like you think that would stop them," muttered Rayne.

"Probably not." The elevator bumped to a stop and the doors opened. "It's showtime, folks" I said and grabbed her ass again.

Rayne let out an eeek and actually jumped an inch or so.

"Christopher, you naughty boy," she said, reaching up to run her fingernail along my cheek. I noticed it was definitely not the one that she had put the drug on. Having me dropping over asleep right now was not part of the plan. Then under her breath she said, *I'm going to get you back for that later.*

At the far end of the lobby, two men, an older and a younger one in Alexander Company security uniforms, sat behind a large desk of monitors. There were three others that were assigned to this shift; they would be off on other floors.

"Hi boys, are we having fun yet?" Rayne said, pulling their attention to her.

"Evening, Mr. Alexander," one of them said, an older fellow with a slight New England accent. "I thought you were in for the evening."

"That was the original plan, Bob." From my research I knew he had been working here for a number of years and he and Christopher were on a semi-friendly basis. "But Ms. Salvatore reminded me of a social obligation that I had forgotten, so we have to venture out for a bit."

"Have a good time, boss," he replied.

I grinned at Rayne, letting my eyes rove all over her. "Oh, I should say so, Bob. Give my regards to your wife."

"I will, sir. Do you want me to wake up your driver and have the car brought round?"

I shook my head. "No need. I'll grab the Ferrari."

Bob cocked his head for a minute, then unlocked a drawer and produced a set of keys that he tossed them to me.

That was when the alarms started going off.

Rayne

When he grabbed my butt as we stepped out of the elevator, it was all I could do to keep from belting him. Zoë Salvatore would not have gone that far; from the way I had built her character these past couple of weeks, she wouldn't have been so crude; sadistic and vengeful maybe, but not crude.

Out of the corner of my eye, I could see the two security guards watching us, or to be more accurate, watching me, which would work. I looked over at the guards and fluttered my eyelids.

"Hi boys, are we having fun yet?"

The younger guard's face flushed red and he got a shit-eating grin on his face when he realized that I was aware of how closely he was watching me. The older-looking guard, who Noah called Bob, just sighed and rolled his eyes skyward.

I had no doubt he was thinking things, not only about my loose morals and loose clothes but how lucky Christopher always seemed to be. Of course, money was probably the best aphrodisiac that he had going beyond his good looks. The younger guard was having his own set of thoughts about me, and it would have been a sure bet that every one of them was x-rated.

We got the keys and were only a few feet from the front door when our carefully laid plan went down the tubes.

A series of loud, blaring alarms sounded from every side of the building. The first words that went through my mind were definitely not ladylike and would have suited the image that the two guards no doubt had in mind for dear little Zoë.

"What in the hell is going on?" yelled Noah.

Maintaining the calm illusion that he was Christopher was now a definite priority and could be the key to saving our skins. Noah held it together.

"I don't know, sir," yelled Bob. "There appear to be multiple security breaches in several different areas at once. Everything seems to be contradicting itself. I'm taking the building to complete lockdown."

"Good. Let me get Ms. Salvatore to a cab first; I want a complete situation report just as soon as I come back through this door."

"But sir...." the younger guard stammered. "In case of lockdown everyone has to remain in the building."

"Don't quote regulations to me," said Noah. "I wrote the damn things! You're fired. Now open these doors."

The younger man's face went pale at those words, not what you want to hear at one in the morning with sirens blaring all around you. The doors remained locked.

Two very large men, and I am talking large, like in front four of the Dallas Cowboys defensive line large, appeared from the elevator at the far end of the lobby. These guys were obviously not from the smile and wave to the public division of Alexander Security, more the 'we're going to kick your ass if we don't like the way you are breathing' part of the organization and it was obvious they were headed right for us.

I figured our cover story was blown to hell and gone so anything I did really didn't matter now. I grabbed a chunky metal plant stand and slammed it hard into the glass door. It didn't break but it did leave an intricate spider web pattern, but the door was still standing. Noah pushed me aside and walloped the door two more times with the metal brief case before it shattered.

If there is one thing I know, it is impossible to run in high heels. So as soon as I was clear of the glass I did the only logical thing, I toed off my sweet kicks and ran barefoot. It hurt my soul to lose those shoes, but the hurt these guys would inflict if they got a hold of us would be a lot worse.

The two of us headed down a small stairwell that led toward the parking garage.

Not far from the stairway I spotted a green door marked maintenance and yanked Noah inside. Thankfully, it wasn't locked. There was a light switch just inside the door. The whole place wasn't much larger than a porta-potty, even though it smelled similar to one. At least we were safe for the moment.

"And this was just going to be a nice easy grab and run," said Noah.

"Tell me about it. So, are you going to quote any odds on us getting away with that?" I pointed at the silver briefcase.

"Stay together; we can do more damage that way," he said.

"Shhh!" Two sets of heavy footfalls went by at high speed.

I scanned the shelves for something that could be used as a weapon. Next to a pile of cleaning rags I spotted someone's pack of cigarettes and a battered old Zippo lighter. I flipped the lid and struck the roller; it sparked and lit right away.

"Not time for a joint right now," said Noah.

"Forget a joint," and I grabbed a spray can marked metal cleaner. "Instant flamethrower."

Noah turned around to survey the rest of what we had to choose from. He found a broken mop handle and held it up. The jagged edges looked deadly enough for our purposes.

"I don't know about you, but I'm good to go."

Noah

I certainly didn't think that it would feel safe hanging out in a parking garage maintenance closet. I've never been that good at doing Magick on the run; I have to take my time. So finding something that could even loosely be called a weapon was a good thing.

"Then let's rock and roll!"

"Did you get a good look at those guys?" asked Rayne as we moved back out into the garage.

"Other than they were massive, menacing and intent on doing us bodily harm, not really. I figure they could have bent us into a pretzel and not even broken a sweat. Was there something else about them I should have noticed?"

"Something didn't feel right about them. I couldn't put my finger on it, but it doesn't matter right now."

The parking area was big and deep, three stories underground, originally designed to support two thousand employees to work in the Alexander building plus visitors, they were never even able to employ two hundred. Nobody wanted to come to Darkness Falls to work. Few of the people who lived here wanted to work either. And nobody came to visit. On the far wall from where we were, I could see a large painted red and white number two. Our ride was waiting on the next level down. The garage was the next thing from dark. What lights that had been built into the place were scattered at long intervals all over the parking level, not creating the best atmosphere in the place.

We passed a few cars as we ran but didn't stop. "You think you could hot-wire one of these?" Rayne asked between gasps.

"Sure, if I had fifteen minutes, a big flashlight and my handy-dandy hot-wiring kit available."

We kept going. As we descended the darkness seemed to intensify. That may have been why I didn't realize that we weren't alone until a hand had grabbed me on the shoulder and jerked me backwards. With the other he dismissed Rayne with a swipe to her head. It was one of the guards. I had no idea where the other was, and right then I didn't care. I had to deal with this hulk.

The man's face was pale, not white like it had been drained of blood, but almost gray like there wasn't any life in him. When he opened his mouth one of the most putrid smells I had ever known came out. The pair of long, large canine fangs that filled his mouth seemed even bigger, as close as he was to me. I bounced the metal case off his head with little effect.

"Damn vampires," I yelled.

He reciprocated my action by throwing me onto the hood of an SUV, my head banging into and splintering the windshield, the briefcase flying away. Lying there, I got a good solid whiff of the rancid breath as he dropped down to bite me. I wedged the broom handle into his jaws preventing them from shutting on my flesh.

Our attacker suddenly turned his attention to Rayne, who had managed to fire up her improvised flamethrower and the sound of whooshing fire. She was forcing him back with it. Vampires aren't the smartest creatures around. Most of them are more like zombies, but the occasional one, like this, was more like a high grade blood sucking pit bull.

Miracle of miracles I came off the car without collapsing. I knew I probably couldn't get close enough to drive the wood stake through his heart, but there were other options. So I threw myself at the ghoul from behind, managing to grab him around the neck and tilt his head up long enough to drive my dagger upwards into his chin and into the brain. Pushing a stake through flesh and bone isn't easy; you have to hope you get it right and slip through the openings that nature left. It was my first time. Beginner's luck.

The vamp shuddered and collapsed backward, carrying me down with him, in maybe ten seconds tops, though it felt more like an hour before that happened. A mixture of blood and some sort of black ichor-like substance came flooding out of the wound and it was coming out all over me. The blood and whatever the other stuff was smelled so bad that it almost made the thing's breath seem minty fresh.

I scrambled to my feet and backed away from the body as it convulsed for another half minute as I caught my wind, then it went quiet. I took a quick glance over my shoulder but the other one was nowhere to be seen,

Rayne was beside me, looking much worse for wear. There was a large bruise under her left eye that I had a feeling was going to be a shiner fairly quickly. She winced slightly when I touched her shoulder.

"You're looking kind of old, Sis. You ok?"

"I'll be alright," she said, handing me the case. I took a knee next to the vamp's body to calm my breathing down.

"What do you think of my new cologne? I call it Odor de Cesspool."

All the stress on the case had popped the locks and torqued the frame of the steel rectangle. I pried it open with my fingers and pulled out a set of papers.

"These are what we really came after? Went through all this?"

"Yup," Rayne said.

I handed them to her so she could examine them and I checked the corpse. There were times I wished these things instantly disintegrated the way they do in the movies and on TV. That would be very convenient. Attached to his belt I found a honking big knife. I stashed the blade through my belt loop and dumped the broken case on the vampire's body.

"Do you have your blow torch?"

"The can's empty. So, why didn't we know that Christopher had vampires on the payroll?" she asked. "Didn't we do all this reconnaissance for a reason?"

"Christopher was never put into a dangerous situation where he had to pull out his secret weapons," I said. "There is only so much you can find out."

I nodded up at the sheets in her hand, "Are we good?"

"Oh yeah! We're good."

"Can we go home now? I would like to survive this evening, if you don't mind."

The two of us limped through the parking level to where our back-up ride was waiting for us. It was a reconditioned Volkswagen van, circa 1968, that, if it had been hand painted, might have looked right at home cruising past the streets of San Francisco. But it was just baby blue and streaked with rust.

"You've got to be kidding me!" Rayne said. "Let me guess; you had a NASCAR motor installed in this thing."

"No, but it's an idea to keep in mind for next time. I've actually never seen this thing before; I just told our associate to find us a ride no one would look twice at and leave it in parking slot F-18."

Only a driver and passenger seat, the rest was open space. The keys were in the visor but it took four tries before the engine finally roared to life, and I've never heard a sweeter sound. I pushed the heater up as far as it would go and put it into drive. The car went nowhere. It was like we were anchored down. As I gave it more gas the wheels squelched and the bus started vibrating. Rayne went back to see what was wrong.

"What the f...."

All at once the back door ripped off and the van leaped forward. Through the rear view mirror I saw that it was in the hand of the second vampire security brute. He threw it away and began running after the car, faster than we were going.

"....uck!"

Rayne

We still had three levels to go through before hitting the street, so we still weren't clear, but I was beginning to feel like things had started to go our way when the engine finally kicked over. But when we weren't moving after a while I got a sinking pit in my gut. It wasn't all the aches and pains I had suffered tonight, it was 'the other shoe is about to drop' sensation. I moved to the rear to see if we were hung up on something.

"What the f...." Noah mumbled when the sound of creaking metal ripped through the hollow back bed of the van. The other guard had caught up with us. He tore the door off its hinges and was charging for the opening, and gaining.

"Noah!?"

The athletic gorilla closed the distance and with Olympic long jump form, leapt and clamped his meaty hands onto the roof, his feet landing on the bumper.

I heard my brother yell, "Rayne! Catch!"

I turned just in time to see the bowie knife he had taken off the other one come flying over his shoulder into the back of the van. I snatched the spinning blade in midair with my right hand, palmed the back of the handle with my left and thrust forward with all my might. Straight into the heart of the vampire. I got sprayed all over my neck and exposed cleavage with the same black gunk that had leaked out onto Noah earlier. The eyes of the demon went wide and burned fire red for just a moment and then he dropped off like a kid jumping backwards into a pool. He bounced twice and rolled to a stop. I made my way up to the passenger seat and collapsed.

"Nice going, Sis," Noah said. "Not bad for an old lady."

"You need some new material. I'm only four minutes older than you," I said.

The difference in our ages was a fact that Noah took perverse pride in reminding me as often as he could find a reason to. It actually didn't bother me all that much anymore, but he expected me to come back at him with a snarky retort. So I did.

I punched him in the face.

He was turning up the loop of the ramp and nearly lost control of the vehicle but corrected quickly.

"If you ever grab my ass again I'll get a knife like the one I just used and decapitate your little dick."

"Would you mind putting any further assaults on hold till we get clear of this place," he said.

"Fine, and we really needed to have a long talk about your choice of transportation."

"What? You don't like it?"

"We could have taken Christopher's Ferrari."

"Oh, shit. In the confusion I forgot I had the keys."

"Dumb-ass."

"Now what? We deliver the documents and go have dinner?" Noah asked as he pulled out of the garage onto the dingy street, narrowly avoiding the blind homeless women that sometimes slept in the alleyway next to the Alexander building. He hung a sharp left and headed for the edge of town.

"Like this?" I exclaimed. "The two of us look like we just capped an oil well and we smell like barbecued skunk. Nobody is going to seat us in this condition."

"McDonald's will."

"That's true, and I am hungry. But not until we get the hell out of Darkness fucking Falls."

About the Authors

BETHANI BRIANNA

Words are like magic- with them you can create anything.

For more writings and artwork by Bethani Brianna you can follow her on Instagram @bethanibrianna

PAUL EAGLE

Paul Eagle was born in England, but has made Canada his home since 2008. He spends his winters living on a Ski Resort in British Columbia with his wife, and they spend their summers working at a children's summer camp in Vermont, USA.

Paul loves seasonal work, as it gives him the chance to enjoy different jobs in different places. Over the last fifteen years Paul has worked as a cleaner in France, a teacher in Korea, a supervisor at an Olympic games and a rugby world cup, and a photographer in a national park.

Paul has a degree in English, a love for Korean food, and a passion for travel.

R. J. ERBACHER

It started with an idea. What if there was this town were dark things happened to people who lived or visited there. From that, a story emerged and developed. Then I thought, how much fun it would be if all kinds of writers had a chance to let their imagination visit this town, each with their own version of events that happened in this malformed community. A vacation spot for the macabre mind. A discussion with a smart editor led to a collaboration and the result is 'Darkness Falls.' A place that you, as an avid reader, might like to wander into and get lost there for a couple of shadowy nights. I hope you enjoy your time in Darkness Falls. I also hope you eventually find your way out.

HENRY VINICIO VALERIO MADRIZ

A Costa Rican teacher who loves Literature and outdoor activities.

BOB MCNEIL

Bob McNeil, writer, editor, cartoonist, and spoken word artist, is the author of Verses of Realness (https://tinylink.net/muF6C). Hal Sirowitz, a former Queens, NY Poet Laureate, called the book "a fantastic trip through the mind of a poet who doesn't flinch at the truth." Among Bob's recent accomplishments, he found working on Lyrics of Mature Hearts to be a humbling experience because of the anthology's talented contributors. Copies of that collection are available here: https://amzn.to/3bU8Loi.

WILLIAM JOHN ROSTRON

William John Rostron is the author of a series of novels steeped in the late 20th and early 21st centuries' music and culture. Band in the Wind, Sound of Redemption, and Brotherhood of Forever have received critical acclaim from Writers Digest, the Online Book Club Review, and many other reviewers. These books have found readership on four continents (North America, Europe, Australia, and Asia). He has been published in fifteen Red Penguin anthologies and four Visible Ink anthologies. The Visible Ink pieces have been produced for the New York stage and are available for viewing on the author's website. www.WilliamJohnRostron.com. An anthology of short pieces entitled A Flamingo Under the Carousel has recently been published by Red Penguin Books.

Born and raised in Queens, NY, William John Rostron now splits his time between his home on Eastern Long Island and traveling the country in his Tiffin motorhome. When not writing, he is busy completing a bucket list of travel adventures. In the past 17 years, he and his wife Marilyn have traveled 140,000 miles. These journeys have taken them to the 48 contiguous states, 133 national parks, all 30 major league baseball stadiums, 154 cities and towns, two Canadian provinces, and a variety of unusual experiences and locations. Many of these locations have served as backgrounds for his books.

He presently working on a fourth novel entitled Lost in the Wind and a second book of short stories.

www.WilliamJohnRostron.com

ELAINE GILMARTIN

I am a therapist by profession, which is actually a great career for writers because I get into people's heads and hear stories that can seem too fantastic even for fiction. It's also helpful in that it is my job to challenge how they perceive themselves and the world around them, not always an easy task! I write regularly on a number of topics for the online site Medium and have self-published a non-fiction book on handling the emotional struggles many faced during the pandemic. I am a member of Women's Fiction Writers and Long Island Authors.

BRADLEY H. SINOR

Bradley H. Sinor, Brad to almost everybody, lives in Tulsa, OK with his wife, Susan P. Sinor and two llarge, economy size cats.

He has previously published several novels and a lot of short stories. The novels include 'The Eye Of Dawn" from Airship 27. "Megan Thomas, Forensic Sorceress," from Eric Flint's Ring Of Fire Press. "The Hunt For The Red Cardinal" with Susan P. Sinor from Eric Flints Ring Of Fire Press. "The Grantville Inquisitor" with Tracy S. Morris from Eric Flint's Ring Of Fire Press.

LIAM A SPINAGE

Liam A Spinage is a former philosophy student, former archaeology educator and former police clerk who spends most of his spare time on the beach gazing up at the sky and across the sea while his imagination runs riot. Occasionally, this imagination has been known to spill out onto paper.

BRIAN STIEGLITZ

Brian Stieglitz grew up in Seaford, New York, and studied Journalism and Creative Writing at Hofstra University. He worked as an editor and columnist at the Long Island Herald and as a reporter for the Daily Mail before transitioning to public relations at ZE Creative Communications, where he currently works. Brian has been an avid fiction writer since childhood and his greatest influences are Stephen King, Clive Barker and Oscar Wilde. His goal as an author is to share LGBTQ+ stories in horror - a genre that has long been a source of comfort and catharsis to queer writers like him.

KELLY ZIMMER

Kelly Zimmer read her first Agatha Christie mystery at age thirteen. She quickly moved on and has lived on a steady diet of murder, thrillers, horror, and suspense novels while laboring in a stifling corporate atmosphere in the wonderfully bizarre and diverse landscape of Florida, USA. She now crafts cozy mysteries and fantasies set in those environments. Her work always includes unlikely protagonists and a touch of humor. Kelly's stories have been featured online and in anthologies.

Visit Kelly on her website at www.kellyzimmerauthor.com, or at her Amazon author page at https://authorcentral.amazon.com/gp/profile.

ALSO FROM THE RED PENGUIN COLLECTION

FICTION

What Lies Beyond – Sci-Fi Stories of the Future

I Can't Find My Flashlight – Contemporary Campfire Stories

A Heart Full of Love – A Collection of Romantic Short Stories

Behind Closed Doors – A Mystery Anthology

Once Upon A Time… – A Fairy Tale Anthology

Ernest Lived …and other Historical Fiction Short Stories

Until Dawn – A Supernatural Anthology

Treat-or-Trick – Halloween Horror Stories

Pets On the Prowl – An Animal Mystery Anthology

My Robot & Me – A Not-So Fiction Anthology

POETRY

Words for the Earth – A Poetry Project

'Tis The Seasons – Poems to Lift Your Holiday Spirits

the flower shop on the corner – A Spring Poetry Anthology

the ocean waves – A Summer Poetry Anthology

the leaves fall – An Autumnal Poetry Anthology

Proud to Be – A Pride Poetry Collection

THE STAND OUT SERIES

Stand Out – The Best of The Red Penguin Collection, Vol. 1

Stand Out – The Best of The Red Penguin Collection, Vol. 2

www.ingramcontent.com/pod-product-compliance
Lightning Source LLC
Chambersburg PA
CBHW050943120626
46552CB00001B/346